I0520359

TERRORIST PLOT

"A Terrorist Deadly Revenge!"

By: G. Prince
"Devoted To Lacing You"

G. Prince
Ghetto Theory Publishing

www.ghettotheorywriting@yahoo.com

Disclaimer

This is a work of absolute fiction! The author has invented and created all of the characters, dialog, and incident, which is purely a product of the author's imagination.

Any resemblance to any actual person's life, or lifestyle; living or dead is purely coincidental, and is not to be associated with the author's imagination, or creative thoughts and expression.

Chapter 1

Detective James Pryor of the Arizona Police Department was driving through traffic on an early morning stake out following a suspected Arms Dealer. The suspected Arms Dealer was in a big black Ford Expedition as he pulled into the parking lot of a park, and pulled next to a brand new S550 Mercedes Benz with two white males wearing sunglasses sitting inside.

Detective James Pryor pulled up and parked on the street adjacent to the parking lot and watched as the suspected Arms Dealer got out of his Ford truck, and walked over to the Mercedes Benz where the two males was parked. One male jumped out of the Benz and walked over to the Ford Expedition and got in, then pulled off as the Arms suspect sat on the passenger side of the Mercedes Benz.

"Damn," Detective James cursed as the Ford Expedition drove out of the parking lot and drove away.

Detective James picked up his walkie-talkie and radio; "this is Detective James Pryor.... I would like to report a black Ford Expedition traveling south on Glendale, possible carrying explosive cargo... pull over and detain, and approach with caution, license plate number 3RPF641, maybe armed and dangerous. I'm in pursuit of other possible suspects. Over!"

The dispatcher responds, "Copy that Detective Pryor.... an APB is out, Over."

The Arms Dealer suspect exited the Mercedes Benz with a leather duffle bag, as he placed it around his shoulder and started walking through the park, as the Benz pulled off and exited the parking lot in the opposite direction. Detective James grabbed his binoculars and looked at the man behind the wheel of the Mercedes Benz, then looked at the back license plate number and seen that it was a Benz dealer advertisement paper plate.

"Damn it!" Detective James said as he pulled into the parking lot of the park and drove onto the grass of the park in hot pursuit of the suspected Arms Dealer.

The suspected Arms Dealer was walking through the park and looked back when he heard a car engine speeding in back of him and he seen a black Dodge Charger coming across the park straight at him with the parking lights flashing, and he broke out running as the Charger swerved on his trail.

The Arms Dealer threw the black duffle bag by some teenagers who was sitting on some park benches, and kept running full speed through the park. The Detective seen that the suspect was getting tired so he skidded to a stop and jumped out of his undercover police cruiser in foot pursuit. Detective James was a track star in his high school years so, he ran the Arms Dealer suspect down with ease. Detective James grabbed the suspect and tackled him as the suspect used the momentum to roll over on top of Detective James, and started swinging wildly at Detective James face striking the Detective multiple times before the Detective was able to wrestle the suspect off, and as the Detective rolled on top of the suspect he started socking the suspect in the face as he held the suspect down.

"Be still... quit fighting! You're under arrest!" The Detective yelled as the suspect squirmed again trying to knock the Detective off, and the Detective socked the suspect two more times in the jaw knocking the suspect unconscious.

"You crazy son-of-a-bitch! I tried to make it easy for you, but you wanted it the hard way." Detective James said as he handcuffed the suspect and looked over by the benches where the suspect threw the black duffle bag, it was gone! The Detective looked toward the far end of the park and seen the teenagers that was sitting on the benches running away with the black duffle bag strapped across their back.

"Damn it! I ought to whoop your ass some more." He said to the suspect as the suspect was shaking his head trying to regain his senses. "You have the right to remaining silent; anything you say will be used against you in a court of law." The Detective picked up the suspect and walked him over to his undercover police car. "You have a right to an attorney, if you cannot afford one then you will be provided a fucked up one to represent you. Do you understand these rights?"

"Fuck you pig!" The suspect muttered.

"I'll take that as a yes! Now what was in the bag?"

The suspect looked over at the park benches where he threw the bag and seen that it was gone and the teenagers that was sitting there was gone too. He started laughing, and said, "What bag?" And started laughing again!

"O'kay Snake, lets see what your real name is?" Detective James took out the suspect wallet and pulled out his ID. "Mr. Jade Abdul, African huh! No wonder why you're so scrappy! Now listen Jade... I'm taken your ass to jail if you don't tell me who was in the black Mercedes Benz, and where did they take the Ford Expedition?"

Jade eyes got big and then he said, "Go fuck yourself!"

"O'kay have it your way." Detective James patted Jade down then put Jade in the passenger seat and put the seat belt around him and drove him to the Police Station.

Ten minutes later they arrived at the Police Station and Detective James walked Jade in through the back-way passing other cops as he nodded and waved. Detective James walked Jade up to the booking counter where Officer Jones was standing behind the counter.

"Hey Detective James who do we have here?" Officer Jones the booking officer asked.

"This is Jade Abdul... say hi Jade!" Detective James joked.

"Fuck you! I know my rights,.. I like to make a phone call, I want to call my attorney!" Jade said in his broken English as he laughed.

"He looks pretty beat up there James!" The booking officer said as he looked at Detective James with a wide eye look.

"Yeah, he attacked me as I tried to arrest him, and I had to restrain him."

"I see! So what do you want to charge him with?"

"Let's start off with resisting arrest and assault on a police officer. I'll add more after I complete my investigation. Ann did you hear anything on the black Ford Expedition that I put an APB on?"

Ann was the booking secretary and she turned and said, "Nothing yet!"

Jade started laughing!

"O'kay let me know once you hear something." Detective James said as he glanced at Jade with a mean look.

"Mr. Jones you got him?"

"Yeah I got him!" The booking officer said as Detective James walked away.

Detective James went to his desk and typed in Jade Abdul name in the identification computer, but his name came up clean. So he did an N.C.I.C. check and nothing came up. "Damn!"

"James!" A officer called out to Detective James as he looked up from his desk. "The Captain wants to see you NOW!"

"Damn! O'kay, o'kay Jim, I'm on my way!" Detective James got up from his desk and walked into the Captains office. "You wanted to see me Captain?"

"Yes...!" Detective Pryor shut the door! Me and Lieutenant Scott here," (he pointed at the Lieutenant that was sitting on the leather couch across from the Captains desk) was sitting here looking at a very interesting video that just went Viral on You Tube, and we were wondering if you could help us understand it?" The Captain hit the remote control to the TV and the scene was being played out of the previous arrest that took place earlier that day with the Arms suspect Jade Abdul, but it only showed part of the incident when Detective James was on top of the suspect socking him in the face.

"Sir., I can explain that! That isn't what really happened."

"Oh it isn't, then why in hell is it all over the damn internet?" The Captain yelled in an angry voice.

"I mean, it's more to the tape... he attacked me first, and I was just defending myself as I tried to gain control of the situation."

"Well Detective, this is the only part that was placed on the internet. Now we got a serious situation, we got a white cop beating a Black Man on tape, and from our point of view, it's not looking good! So if you got some hard evidence on this person or serious charges, then now will be the time to share it.

"Well Sir., I was conducting surveillance on Mr. Jade Abdul because I got word from a reliable confidential informant that Mr. Jade Abdul a.k.a. Snake was a big time Arms Dealer. So I was following him today when he went to the park on the Southside, and met with two white males driving a brand new S550 Mercedes Benz. Mr. Abdul was in a black Ford Expedition truck and when he arrived at the park he got out and went to go speak with the two white males in the Mercedes. Then the white male who was on the passenger side got out and went over to the Ford Expedition and drove off. I called it in and the dispatcher put and APB out on the truck."

"Did the suspect in the truck get pulled over and detained?" The lieutenant asked.

"No Sir. Not yet!"

"Continue Detective!" The Captain ordered.

"Well, after the truck drove off the suspect Abdul jumped into the passenger side of the Benz, then three minutes later exited with a big black duffle bag and started walking through the park as the Mercedes drove off. The black Mercedes had dealer's license plates so I couldn't call it in, so I chose to pursue the suspect Abdul as he headed through the park. I drove through the park to catch up with him and he started running when he saw me coming. He then threw the black duffle bag by some teenagers sitting on some park benches and kept running trying to get away. I jumped out of my car and started to pursue the suspect on foot. I yelled for him to stop and identified myself as the police, and he kept running so I tackled him and he ended up on top of me and started socking me in my face. 'See the marks,' (the detective showed the red marks and scratches then continued telling his story) so I rolled the suspect off of me and he was still fighting so I hit him back to try to subdue him. But he kept fighting, so I hit him again and knock him unconscious, then rolled him over and handcuffed him."

"Did you get the duffle bag?" The Lieutenant asked.

"No, the teenagers that were sitting at the park on the benches, pick it up and ran off with it when I was trying to detain the suspect."

"So let me get this straight! You didn't get no weapons, you didn't get the Ford truck, you didn't get the suspect who was in the Mercedes, you didn't get the black duffle bag, and you're on tape beating the crap out of a black suspect, who I've been informed has no criminal history, nor do we have any evidence to collaborate your story. Did you by any chance take photos of the suspect or the vehicles?"

"No Sir!"

"Well Detective Pryor, you're a fine Detective and I believe that you've just became a victim of circumstances. But unfortunately, I have to suspend you pending further investigation."

"Captain, I'm being set up!"

"I understand this son, me and your father were the best of friends and partners before he passed, and it doesn't do my heart justice to have to make such a decision. But considering the Media's attention that we're about to receive, and the possible law suit that will be filed, I have no other choice! I have to secure the integrity of the precinct. I will not dock your pay, but know that this is pending Internal Affairs review."

The Captains door swung open and the Governor of Arizona walked in.

"Jim," the Captain said as he stood up at attention!

"Captain Fields, I can't begin to tell you how devastated I am about this video that just went Viral," the Governor said.

"I understand Sir., and I was just scolding Detective Pryor here on how his behavior is frowned upon, I suspended him pending further investigation," the Captain said.

"Suspended! Oh no my good friend, Detective Pryor is fired pending criminal investigation!" The Governor firmly stated.

"Sir., Jim! Isn't that being too harsh? We haven't really had a chance to investigate the situation yet."

"Captain Fields, we are having the Grand Opening of one of the biggest Casinos in the world, and the President of the United States will be attending this Grand Opening with esteem Leaders and Aristocrats from all over the world for a signing of the Anti-Terrorism International Peace Union. Do you think for one minute that I would allow one of my officers to get away with this type of behavior on my watch? This barbaric act can cause an uprising and ruin everything that we have worked hard to bring about. I'll tell you what he better be happy for, he better be happy that he's not in handcuffs! Now turn in your badge and service pistol, and hope that this incident doesn't cause any racial conflict. I know that Al Sharpton is probably on his way down here as we speak!"

Detective Pryor eyes was blood shot red, as he took off his badge and gun and walked out of the office. Everyone was staring at him as he walked back to clean out his desk and left the precinct.

Chapter 2

The next day James Pryor was sitting in his lazy boy recliner drunk off a bottle of Johnny Walker Red when he heard a knock at the door. He looked over at the clock on the wall and it read 6:15 p.m.

"Who is it?"

"It's me Janet, open up this door boy!"

Janet was James god sister. James father use to date Janet's mother when they were in middle school. James use to run off Janet's boyfriends and take up for her like a big brother. The only odd issue was that James was white and Janet was black, so James had his work cut out for him, but he will always rise to the occasion, nevertheless; they where brother and sister and no one could tell them otherwise.

James staggered to the door and opened it and said, "Hey Sis, long time no see," and gave her a hug and a kiss on the cheek.

"Uh, Uh! I know you're not laying-up in here in the dark drinking yourself crazy! James you're better than this!"

"I've been crossed out Sis, he hit me first when I was trying to detain him. I was just defending myself."

James slurred as he raised his shoulder and arms, then dropped them to his side, as if to say, 'I give up!'

"I know big bro, but you can't let this break you." Janet said as she gently grabbed the sides of his face with her hands and looked him straight in his eyes.

"But that fat muthafucka fired me.... the Governor Sis, the Governor fired me!" James slurred as he shook his head and walked over to the Lazy Boy recliner and sat down, then grabbed his bottle of whisky and tried to drink it, as Janet snatched the bottle away.

"Not this way James!"

"Girl give me my bottle back!"

"NO, now get your ass up!"

"For what?" James asked with a frown on his face.

"Because you need a cold shower."

"I'm not taking a damn shower...!"

"Get your butt up now!" Janet yelled as she slapped him hard on the leg.

"Stop girl, quit playing." James said as he laughed.

"I said get up!" Janet said firmly as she twisted his ear like she would always do when they were young.

"O'kay, o'kay, stop twisting my ear!" James whined as Janet lead him to the shower by his ear.

She cut on the cold water to the shower while holding his ear as he laughed and whined like a big kid.

"Now get in there!" Janet ordered.

"Hell naw, that shit is cold!" James fussed.

"I said get your stinky butt in there now...!" Janet yelled as she twisted his ear again.

"O'kay, O'kay!" James said as he jumped in the shower fully dressed. "This shit is cold." James said with a whiny voice.

"Shut up that damn whining, and don't come out until you get that stank up off you. I'll sit you some clothes out on the bed, and I'm gonna fix you something to eat."

James started throwing up in the shower. As Janet shook her head and walked out laughing.

James lost his mother when he was five years old, so when his father and Janet's mother started dating, then James became Janet little bad brother, and even thought they were only a year apart, there love and bound was priceless because they both fulfilled each-other's void.

James walked into the kitchen and sat at the dining room table looking like a different person.

"O'kay now, that's the man that I know." Janet said with a cheerful smile as she sat a plate with a fat steak, butter corn, and French fries on it.

James looked up and smiled, because this was always his childhood favorite meal. "Think you big sis!" James said as he put salt and ketchup on his food and started eating.

Janet sat a glass of Cherry kool-aid next to him and sat down in the chair.

"James, I know how much you like being a cop and catching bad guys and all, but it's time to move on to something better. Something more secure and less dangerous and I got the perfect job for you." James looked up as he was chewing his food. I told my new boss Mr. Kerr at the new Casino that's opening about you and your situation, and he said that he'll give you a job on his security staff. He said that he can use a man with your experience and perception."

"Does he know that I just got fired because of a police brutality issue?"

"Sure he knows! Who don't know....? You've been all over the News for the last 24 hours." Janet said as she laughed.

James smiled, "And he's still gonna hire me after that?"

"Well, he said that he'll do it for me! I think that he got the hot's for me." Janet said with a shy grin.

"Don't make me whoop his ass girl!"

"You better not James!" Janet said as she socked him in the shoulder.

"You like him too don't you?" James asked after seeing that twinkle in Janet eyes.

"He's cute, but he's much older than me."

"How much older?"

"He's about 60 or so!" Janet said as she squeezed her face trying to look innocent.

"You scandalous little helfa! You're dating an old rich Viagra pill poppin son of a gun." James joked as they laughed.

"No we're not dating, we're just friends." Janet said in her defense.

"What nationality is he?" James asked.

"I don't know, I think that he's an East Indian or something."

"A towel head...? Yeah, he got money!" James said as they laughed.

"So you'll take the job?"

"Well, it looks like I got to or I'm gonna be sleeping on your couch, and you know that I'm not trying to deal with your crazy bossy ass!" And they both started laughing.

"I'm not crazy....you're the one who's a bit crazy. But you got to be professional with this job. The grand opening is in two days, and the President of the United States will be hosting his Anti-Terrorism International Peace Union, and Leaders, Diplomats, and Aristocrats from all over the world would be attending. So please don't mess this up! There will be Secret Service Officers all over the place not including all of the Security Guards that will be watching over all of the International Leaders. So be on your best behavior o'kay, and soon all of this police brutality stuff will be long forgotten, Promise!"

Janet held out her pinkie finger and James held his pinkie finger out, and they intertwined them like when they we're kids. "O'kay, I'll see you tomorrow morning 8:00 a.m. and don't be late."

"I won't, and thank you Sis." James said.

Janet smiled and said, "That's what family is for!" Then moved over and kissed him on his cheek as she got up and left.

James smiled and went and laid down.

* * * *

The following day James was dressed in his best dark blue suit as he walked into the New Casino doors at 7:50 a.m.   He was mesmerized by all of the black and white marble décor with gold trimming everywhere.

"Mr. Pryor I presume?" An older White Man asked as he approached James.

"Yes Sir., how are you doing?"   James asked as they shook hands.

"My name is Mr. Adam White, I'm the Executive Security Manager here at the Gold Stallion."

"It's a pleasure to meet you Sir!" James said.

"No the pleasure is all mines! I heard a lot of interesting things about you. But, nothing is of concern at this point. Everyone is entitled to a mistake once in their life, but let's make sure that it doesn't happen twice o'kay?" Mr. White looked James in the eyes with a stern look.

"Yes Sir., I understand and I promise you it won't happen again." James said as he stared back into Mr. White eyes.

"Good, good, I believe you. Your sister speaks very highly of you, and by your previous Military history, I believe that you could be an asset to our Corporation. I understand that you did a six year tour in the Marines prior to your five years in the Police Academy."

"Yes! I spent two years in Iraq and two years in Afghanistan in a special combat unit." James said as they started walking toward the elevators.

"Sounds interesting, and it's good to see that you've came back in one piece. I hope that we don't have to worry about a flash back once our Middle East Associates arrive?" Mr. White said as he turned to look at James in the elevator right before the doors closed.

"No Sir., I'm mentally sane and stable." James said with a smile as he laughed at the humor.

"Good, good! Everyone is not so enthused over your presence here. My constituents seem to question your stability to perform around such stuck up, rich, and powerful people with attitudes. I'm sure you recognize that it takes a lot of tolerance and diplomacy to deal with certain types of egos. However, (the elevator opened up and they walked out as Mr. White lead the way) Mr. Kerr seems to favor your presence, and that's all that matters....because he's the, shall we say; 'Shot Caller.' Therefore, if my constituents seem to give you a hard time or act funny, then you know why." Mr. White opened up a big door to a conference room and four men were sitting at the big oval table. "Gentlemen, I'd like you to meet Mr. Pryor!" Mr. White said as they entered, and he closed the door to the conference room.

"Oh Mr. Pryor, there you are....it's a pleasure to meet you! Janet speaks very highly of you. Please have a seat! My name is Mr. Kerr and I'm the owner of this fine establishment." An older looking East Indian man said as he shook James hand.

"The pleasures mine Sir., and thank you for this opportunity," James said.

"It's nothing; everyone deserves a chance to show their true nature. These are four of my Executive Security Team. You've met Mr. White he oversees our retail... our restaurants, boutiques, fitness center, and salons. Mr. Caly here deals with security over our entertainment events, Mr. Faller deals with our Casino Security Division. And last but never least, Mr. Quick who oversees our Financial and Banking System." (Another younger East Indian man walked in and closed the door behind himself.) "Oh Cin, glad you can make it! Cin, this is Mr. Pryor he will be on your Security Team, so make sure you brief him well. Mr. Pryor, this is my nephew Cin, he's the head over our security employees."

James got up and shook his hand, "Please to meet you Mr. Cin."

"It's good to meet you too, I seen your video, kind of extreme but effective and hopefully was necessary," Cin said.

"Yes it was!"

"Good, but tone it down for us here, these are the good crooks." Cin said as everyone started laughing.

"Mr. Pryor are you still licensed to carry a gun?" Mr. Kerr asked.

"Yes Sir." James replied.

"Good, you will be required to carry your firearm here, but keep it conceal at all times and only use it in a life or death situation, understand?" Mr. Kerr said.

"Yes Sir., I understand!"

"Sir., I don't think that that's a good idea!" Mr. Quick interjected.

"Oh don't worry, Mr. Pryor will be fine."

Mr. Kerr said to Mr. Quick. "Cin why don't you go show Mr. Pryor around our lovely Casino. Take him down to Mr. Lee to get fitted with some nice suits. Image is everything, and here at the Gold Stallion we represent elegance, so always keep your attire nice. Oh, and before he leaves take him down to Personnel so he can fill out the necessary paperwork."

"O'kay Sir.! Cin said as they stood up.

"And Mr. Pryor!" Mr. Kerr said.

"Yes!"

"Welcome aboard!" Mr. Kerr said with a gentle smile.

"Thank you sir, and I won't let you down!" James replied.

"I know!" Mr. Kerr said as James and Cin walked out.

James looked over at Cin as they were headed for the elevator and seen that he was only about 26 years old.

"O'kay, check it out James, we'll start with the 10th floor where our main security station is. This place is one of the biggest Casino built in the United States. We got over 600 luxury rooms and 100 elegant suites (they got in the elevator) now the Casino is 25 stories high, and over 120,000 square feet of enjoyment space. We host 2500 of the newest slot machines, 150 gaming tables, 30 poker tables with 15 private high stake poker rooms. (They exist the elevator and headed down the hall,) 3 sport lounges complete with private bars, 4 spas, 3 salons, 2 barber shops, a state of the art fitness centers, every relevant retail shop that you can think of, an 18 hole golf course, and 3 theatres plus, a ball room that highlights an A- List entertainment. And most important this! (Cin used his key card to open a big bullet proof glass door and they walked in.) A fifty million dollar state of the art computer system that's equipped with facial recognition, thermal scope, and info red laser beams, this system has been certified as hack proof. Mr. Quick hired 3 of the best hackers in the world to try to penetrate the system, and offered them a two million dollar grand prize to anyone of them who could successfully hack through this system. And they all failed! But my uncle hired them to oversee certain operation of the system. But not the banking part, that's only overseen by Mr. Quick and his Private Personnel. Each of them has to have special clearance, because the banking system is so high tech. It's all electronic transaction and it connects to other banks through one electronic service, so any one of our customer can wire millions of dollars to our Casino for their gambling and spending pleasures within minutes. What do you think of that? Very sophisticated huh!"

"It sounds sophisticated!" James said.

"Hey Bill, come here for a second." Cin called out as a young Black Man walked up.

"What's up Cin?" Bill said as he approached them with a smile on his face while eating a sandwich.

"This is Mr. Pryor one of my new security. He'll have clearance so you'll be seeing him around," Cin said.

"O'kay, what's up Mr. Pryor if you need anything, just holla." Bill said.

"Thanks a lot.... I will," James replied.

"Well let's roll, I got to show you the rest of the place. Catch you later Bill." Cin said.

"Later!" Bill said as Cin and James turned and walked away.

"He's pretty cool! That's one of the hackers that I was telling you about. Come on we got a long day ahead of us." Cin said as they entered the elevator.

* * * *

James got home at 8:15 p.m. and was exhausted. He put his new clothes up and sat in his lazy boy recliner with his Carl's Jr. Hamburger and fries when the phone rang.

"Hello!"

"How did it go today?" Janet asked as James picked up the phone.

"It was interesting! That place is amazing and huge! I got lost twice." James said as they laughed.

"So you like it?"

"It's different, but it's nice being around all that expensive and lavish stuff. It's gonna take some getting use to, and they pay better then the police department." (They both laughed)

"I'm glad that you liked it!"

"Yeah, and your boyfriend brought me some new clothes. I like him, you should keep him." James laughed.

"Bye James! See you tomorrow!"

"O'kay Sis., bye and thank you!"

"You're welcome...sleep tight!" (click, they hung up.)

James smiled and cut on the basketball game as he relaxed, enjoying his food.

Chapter 3

The next day James walked into the Casino at 6:50 in the morning and the place was wide awake. Everyone who was there was working hard making last minute arrangements and other employees were arriving on the minute.

"Hey James, hope you had a good night rest, because we have a long day planned. Nice suit, you're looking pretty G.Q. today." Cin said with a friendly smile as he shook James hand.

"Thank you!" James replied.

"O'kay, now we got a meeting in the ball room at 7:30 a.m. sharp, so don't get lost. The ball room is on the 12th floor. Now go and clock in and mingle while I finish up here. No Margaret not there, put the gold roses around the check-in desk." Cin said as he walked away.

James headed for the staff lounge so he could clock in on time. The staff lounge was crowed as James scanned the crowd looking at all of the beautiful women who worked at the Casino with him. "Now this is gonna be fun," James said to himself as he clocked in then turned around and accidentally bump into this cute blonde hair woman with a sexy tan. "Pardon me!" James said with a player's smile.

"Oh, that was my fault! I was looking in my bag trying to grab my employee's ID card. My name is Cindy!" The pretty white girl said with a flirtatious smile.

"Please to meet you, my name is James!" James said as they shook hands.

"What do you do here James?"

"I work security here, and you?"

"Oh, I'm a Black Jack dealer."

"Sounds like fun," James said.

"Well, it has its times!" And they both started laughing together.

"Well, I'll see you around then!"

"O'kay, nice to meet you," Cindy said.

"You too!" James said as he smile and headed for the door and all the women were hawking him.

James went toward the elevators and ran into two big black dudes, the biggest one he knew very well.

"Well, well, what do we have here? Detective Pryor...! Long time no-see!" The big muscular built black dude said.

"John Franks a.k.a. Big Ace, so they finally let your ass out of prison huh!" James said in a condescending tone.

"Of course, they can't keep a good brotha' down for ever. I seen you on the News the other day, and heard that they suspended your punk ass!" Big Ace said as he and his partner laughed.

"Oh snap, that's the pig that was on the News the other day, the one who beat-up the young brotha', dirty muthafucka!" The short brown skin brotha' said.

"What they let your bitch out of prison with you, and ya'll casing out the joint or something?" James said.

"Oh you got jokes huh white boy!" Big Ace said.

"I got your bitch white boy!" The short brotha interjected.

"Be cool Sammy, not at work!" Big Ace told his short buddy.

"Oh, you and Sammy work here too?" James asked.

"Yeah it's called equal opportunity white boy. Mr. Kerr believes that a person should have a second chance, so he has a ex-con program." Big Ace said.

"What do ya'll do?"

"We're Bell Boys!" Big Ace said as him and Sammy gave each other dap. "What about you...? You here for a job or something?"

"I hope he don't hire your punk ass!" Sammy said as he looked at James in the eyes!

"Well as a matter of fact, I'm the security here, so know that I'm gonna be watching you both!" James said as he laughed and walked into the elevator, then put his two fingers up to his eyes, and pointer to both of them as the elevator door closed.

"Damn man, it's our first day and you already got the police on our line. I'm gonna have to shake your ass, you're hot as a muthafucka." Sammy said as he shook his head.

"Man don't trip that fool, he got too many other issues to worry about. We're the last thing on his mind. Hell, they're talking about indicting his punk ass... he might be somebody's bitch pretty soon!" And they both laughed.

"You ain't lying remember what happened to Officer Joe Cruz when he hit the pound?" Sammy said.

"Yeah, how can I forget, I think every white boy on the prison yard either beat him up, or violated him." Big Ace said as they laughed.

Come on, let's go to the theatre and flirt with the show girls!"

"Hell yeah, let's roll!" Big Ace said as they took off toward the theatre.

* * * *

James stepped off the elevator on the 12th floor and followed a small crowd into the elegant ball room. The place was packed with about 50 security staff some able to carry firearms, and some was just trained unarmed security look outs. The men out numbered the women 70/30 and about 25 security men were gathered off to the side of the ball room like they had their own special clique. About 15 middle eastern and 8 whites and two blacks. But they all looked like they were military trained by the way they walked and stood at attention. But on the other side of the ball room, it was like 15 women of all nationalities and 5 white men, 2 Mexicans, and 3 blacks, and they all looked like college students and rookies. James laughed to himself and walked over toward the group of ladies.

"Hi there, my nane is Barbra, and this is Ann and Toni." A tall cute white lady with brunette hair said, as she introduced herself to him and her friends.

"Hello Ladies It's a pleasure to meet you, my name is James."

"Hi James!" The two other ladies said.

"Excuse me Sir!" A tall White Man said as he walked up to James with two other men, a Mexican and a black.

"Yes?" James said as he turned away from the ladies.

"Are you James Pryor?" The tall White Man asked.

"Yes I am, how can I help you." James said as he was thrown off guard by the question.

"I told you! This is the policeman that just whooped that black dude ass on TV, I never forget a face now pay up!" The Mexican and Black Man reached in their pocket and both handed the tall White Man a $20 dollar bill, as everybody around them started whispering and James face turned red from embarrassment.

"Please be seated so we can begin." Cin announced over the microphone. James let out a silent breath as he hurried to a seat. Mr. Faller and Mr. Quick was sitting down on the stage as Mr. Cin stood over the microphone at the podium.

"I'm proud to announce that tomorrow will be the Grand Opening of the first Gold Stallion Casino lounge."

(And everyone stood up and applauded.)

"All of you have been chosen respectfully, to watch over and represent this fine establishment from any trouble or problems that may arrive, but I ask that you perform your duties diligently, respectfully, and with diplomacy, not with violence or aggression." And the tall White Man and his crew looked over at James and laughed. James looked at them like they were crazy and then ignored them.

"Ladies and gentlemen, we will be honoring the President of the United States and other elite Leaders and guest from all over the world, and they all will be in attendance with their own special armed Security Team as well as Secret Service Agents and maybe FBI. So don't be alarmed by the different Security Teams and how they move, just be polite and understanding, and I'm sure we will have a profitable and pleasant Grand Opening. Now, in here lays our Security Team. Please become acquainted and familiar with everyone's appearance. We're expecting a very big crowd for this event, so you can expect to work overtime and find a handsome bonus on your first pay check." (and everyone started applauding.)

"Now I will turn it over to my boss Mr. Faller."

"Thank you, Mr. Cin has covered my concerns well. But, I could never state enough on how important it is for all of you to be very professional in dealing with this crowd. These will be some of the world's wealthiest elites, and influential politicians of today's time. That means you'll be dealing with the most conceited, craziest, self-centered, spoil brats in the world, and they all have an entourage of security around them making them look more important. It's like all of the big wigs in the world coming here to have a pissing contest, and hundreds of thousands of dollars will be thrown around like pennies. So it's up to us to tolerate the non-sense so they can floss and enjoy playing their games. You have a job to do, so make sure that you do your job well and be professional and courteous. Now we have personal two-way radios that we will be using to converse between one another. We will use different codes among our Security Team. A black horse means a minor incident requesting executive staff assistance. A red horse means that there's a big problem and everyone must converge onto the location immediately. This will provide the added assistance needed to contain any problem before it gets out of hand. If you neglect to converge during this type of incident, then your job will be in jeopardy. So understand how important this is! All two-way radios will be turned to station 8 at all times. Remember your routes, and if you have any questions or problems, then you can consult with any of the Security Team with the Gold Handkerchief, they are part of our head management group. With that said, you can come up and get your two-way radios. Thank you!" Mr. Faller said as everyone got up and went to grab their walkie-talkies.

After the meeting, James became acquainted with the majority of the security staff. However, the one's that wore the gold handkerchiefs was acting like they were too good to acknowledge him. He didn't know if it was their eastern character trait, or they just didn't care to meet him, either or, it didn't matter. Mr. Faller and Mr. Quick obviously handpicked them and brung them from the Mesopotamia Region, because they all resemble one another. James contemplated his thoughts as he went on his designated route, then went to explore the Casino and its amenities.

An hour later he located the Accounting Office on the basement ground floor, right next to were the big electronic banking system is located. James showed his security badge and walked in to go see his sister.

"Excuse me, is Ms. Janet Mills in?" James inquired.

"Just one minute Sir., what's your name?" The heavy set black secretary asked.

"My name is James, I'm her brother."

"Of course, I can see the resemblance!" The secretary said with a fake smile, and James just laughed and shook his head, knowing that no one ever believed him, because of the white and black thang. "Excuse me Ms. Mills, you have a Mr. James out here requesting to see you. Yes, I'll tell him." (Click she hung up the phone.) You can have a seat; she said that she'll be out in a minute."

"Thank you Maam!"

Janet came out 5 minutes later and she gave James a big hug and kiss on the cheek. "Look at you looking all sophisticated up in here."

"You like it?" James asked with a big smile on his face as he gave a G. Q. pose.

"Of course, you look like a G. Q. model..! I know that all of these ladies is jocken them some you." Janet teased then turned to the black heavy set secretary and said, "Oh Linn, I like you to meet my brother James, James this is my good friend Linn."

James smiled and said, "I told you so!" Then he and Janet started laughing but, Linn had a confused look on her face.

"Well it's nice to meet you Mr. James."

"The pleasure is all mines!"

"Come on into my office." Janet said as she pulled James by the arm.

"You got an office?" They walked into Janet's private offices. "Dame Girl you'll doing big thang's around here. Is this Real gold?" James pointed to the Gold Stallion statute that was on her desk.

"Yes, it's the Casino trademark. All of the Executive Offices have them," Janet said.

"So how do you like the job?"

"I like it a lot! But, there's some funny style people here that I don't care for, but for the most part, it's great!" (They both laughed.) "So what's up with Mr. Faller and Mr. Quick? They act like they don't like me! Therefore, the other East Indians on the Security Team is acting funny too!"

"Don't worry about them, you just do your job and they'll come around. You just probably have to prove yourself. That's all!" Janet encouraged.

"Well, if that's all it is, then I got this!"

"I know you do, and you better get you a good night sleep tonight, because this place will be jumping like New Years Eve tomorrow, and we're gonna be working a double-double shift." Janet said.

"You're probably right! Let me get out of here so I can get ready for tomorrow."

"O'kay big bro, love you!"

"I love you too!" James said as he hugged Janet and kissed her on her forehead and left out."

Chapter 4

James walked thru the two big bullet-proof double doors at 6:45 a.m., as he entered into the Gold Stallion Casino lounge red carpet.

"What's up James, I see that you're up bright and early this morning." Cin said as he gave a warm smile and shook his hand.

"Top of the morning to you too! I was wondering do you ever sleep?" James joked.

"No, Why? I'll sleep when I'm dead. Ha, ha!" They laughed. "Oh here she is, Debbie come here sweetheart." A beautiful Egyptian looking woman walked up wearing an elegant expensive white skirt-suit, and it was hugging the curves of her sexy figure like she was born in it. "Close your mouth James!" Cin whispered as he said, "Debbie I like you to meet Mr. James Pryor, he's a part of my Security Team, so if you need him, then just call for him. James this is Debbie Tubae, our Executive Concierge! Nothing would move without her."

"Oh Cin, your much too modest. It's good to meet you Mr. Pryor."

"Please call me James and the pleasure is all mine's."

"Nice suit!" Debbie said as she smiled and walked away.

Cin and James were hypnotized by her sexy looking ass. She looked back at them and they didn't even act like they weren't looking at her butt. She just smile and kept walking.

"Damn, she's beautiful! What nationality is she?" James asked.

"Who care's! She could be a damn Alien and nobody would care, she's so fine!" Cin joked.

"You ain't lying, I'd chase her fine ass from planet to planet James said as they gave each other dap and laughed. "Cin, what's up with these entrance ways? Two double doors and bullet proof glass. Isn't that a bit extreme?" James asked.

"No my friend, we need tight security here. It's a lot of money in here and Mr. Quick insisted that we have these computerized state of the art bullet proof doors put in. See the computer system can control them, so if a robbery should occur, then once the robbers exit thru the first double doors, then the computer system will lock them in the foyer part in-between both bullet proof doors." Cin explained.

"I guess that that's kind of smart!" James said.

Well, the doors open for the public at 8:00 a.m. sharp, so go get you some breakfast in the staff lounge so you can have a full tank!" Cin said with a smile.

"Sounds good, I'll see you in a minute, and if you need me then hit me up on the radio."

"Will do!" Cin said as James strolled off.

James went and grabbed an egg, cheese and bacon sandwich with orange juice and went and did a last minute check on his rounds.

"Hey Detective Pryor!" James looked to his left toward the bathroom entrance, and seen Big Ace and Sammy standing there with two other white boys with gold Bell Boy jackets on. "I heard that they're about to indict you on the racial abuse case, if you want me to, I'll holler at one of my friends in prison and tell them to look after that ass!" And Big Ace and his crew started rolling.

"James just smiled and kept walking as he shook his head. He went up stairs to the top floor where the $25,000 dollars a night elegant suites where overlooking the golf course on one side, and the pool and tennis courts area on the other. As he walked by the first suite he seen that the door was cracked, so he pushed the door open and glance in and said "Damn!"

Ms. Debbie Tubae was on her hands and knees on the plush carpet looking for something but her ass was pointed to the door. "Excuse me!" Debbie said as she looked back.

"Oh, did I say that out loud? My bad! I almost tripped that's all." James said in his defense. "What's wrong did you lose something?" James said as he walked up.

"Yeah my diamond earring fell off somewhere around here, and I was looking for it."

James seen a sparkle in the plush carpet by the edge of the leather love seat and said, "Is this it?" As he reached down and picked up the expensive diamond princess cut earring.

"Yes that's it! Thank you very much I appreciate it." Debbie said with a flawless smile.

"I'm glad that I could be of service!" James smiled as she blushed. "Can I ask you a little personal question?"

"Depends!" Debbie said as she arched her eye brow.

"No, it's nothing like that! All I wanted to know was what nationality are you?" James asked

"My mother is Egyptian and my father is Puerto Rican, so that makes me half Egyptian and half Puerto Rican." Debbie said with a smile.

"That has to be one of the most erotic combinations ever created, because you are hypnotic!" James said as he gazed spell bound into her beauty.

"James are you flirting with me?"

"Not if it would get me in trouble, but believe me I want too!" James said as they laughed.

"Aren't you Janet brother?"

"Yes, can't you see the family resemblance?" James gave his best player pose.

"Not really!" Debbie said as they both started busting up laughing.

"Well, I better get back to work, it's been a pleasure, hopefully we can do this again sometime." James said.

"Maybe!" Debbie said in a nonchalant way then James smiled and walked out, he turn and glanced back to see if she was still staring at him, and when their eyes met, Debbie blushed as James grin and headed back down stairs.

Mr. Kerr cut the gold ribbon at 8:00 o'clock on the dot, and the doors were open for business. Limousines and taxies pulled up by the droves, and helicopters started flying in two at a time.

"Damn look at that one! Now she's baaadd! With a double D, and I do mean double D's" Big Ace said as him and his little crew of Bell Boys stood to the side waiting for the Maitre d' to call them to help the guest with their suit cases.

"Scott can you please come and help Mr. and Mrs. Thomas to their room?" The Maitre d' Tammy asked.

"Damn, Scott silently cursed as everyone gave a brief chuckle.

"Look at this beautiful specimen here! She got to be Ms. Canada or someone." Sammy said as they all hawked at the Canadian bomb shell.

"You ain't lying she's gorgeous!" Tom said as Big Ace and Sammy looked at him crazy. "What?" Tom asked.

"Don't no body use gorgeous any more. You sound like a nerd!" Big Ace said as him and Sammy laughed.

"Either that big buff dude is her husband, or her bodyguard." Sammy said.

"Yeah, he look's kind of like that big Russian dude that was on Rocky IV," Tom said.

"Yeah, that got to be her bodyguard the way he's posted up." Big Ace said.

"Sammy can you help Ms. Birch with her luggage please." Tammy called out.

"Why sure!" Sammy said as he smiled at Big Ace.

"Lucky Bastard." Big Ace whispered as Sammy walked away.

"James can you report to the top floor A-1 helicopter pad?" Cin called over the two-way radio.

"Copy Sir, I'm on my way." James said as he walked over and got into the elevator.

The elevator door was about to close when Sammy yelled out, "hold that door please!" And the elevator operator opened the door back up. Sammy walked in with three big suit cases and the Canadian lady and her body guard walked in behind him. Sammy said, "the twentieth floor please," and old man Joe the elevator operator pushed the button as the door closed. James saw the Canadian lady's reflection off the elevator shiny door as the lady looked him up and down in a flirtatious way. James glance at her and smiled.

"Hi there?" the Canadian lady said.

"Hello, how do you like the Casino?" James asked trying to be polite.

"It's amazing! I can't wait to see more. Do you work here?" She asked.

"Yes, I'm the security here at the Casino."

"Oh that's great, I feel a lot safer now." She flirted as the bodyguard and Sammy let out a small chuckle.

"What-cha' laughing for? He's so cute and strong looking." The bodyguard and Sammy started busting up again.

"Oh you like to laugh huh, well laugh at me when I give you a tip, little funny man!" Sammy stop laughing as his eyes got big and James, Joe, and the bodyguard started busting up as the elevator door opened to the twentieth floor. The Canadian lady turned toward James and said, "I'll see you around o'kay!"

"O'kay, enjoy your stay!" James said.

"I plan too!" She said as the door closed.

"That's an untamed lioness. Son, you better watch out she's on the prowl and you're the prey," Joe said as they both laughed and the elevator door opened up.

"Thanks old timer" James said.

"Anytime, have a nice day now," Joe said as he laughed and the elevator door closed.

James walked around to the A-1 helicopter pad where Cin and a couple other securities were waiting. Two helicopters were closing in, in the distance.

"Hey stud, you almost missed the big event." Cin said with a smile.

"Oh yeah, who is that?" James asked.

"He's the nephew of the Sheikh of Saudi Arabia. He wired 5 million into the Casino account for his weekend expenses.

Three helicopters landed one behind the other and 4 armed guards exited the first helicopter, and another 4 guards exited out of the second helicopter as the Sheikh's nephew exited out of the third helicopter with three more armed guards on his side, and they all carried AR-15 automatic rifles, and four of them grabbed two large trunks out of the helicopter private department and carried it as they where approached by Mr. Kerr and Ms. Debbie.

"It's an honor Mr. Muti, welcome to the grand opening of our elegant Casino the Gold Stallion." Mr. Kerr said as Mr. Muti just smiled. Mr. Muti and his body guards all wore their Muslim head garbs and sun glasses so it was hard to tell their expression. "Well, Ms. Tubae here is our executive concierge and she will show you to your executive suites and make sure that your accommodations are up to par. We prepared four of our most luxurious suites for you and your associates on the 23 floor. Ms. Tubae will escort you there, and assist you with anything that you might need."

"Thank you!" Mr. Muti said as he turned towards Ms. Tubae as she turned and lead the way toward the entrance to the casino.

* * * *

"Bill what do you think that you're doing?" Mr. Quick screamed at Bill the computer specialist.

"I was just trying to get a facial recognition on the Sheikh's nephew." Bill said as he sat at his computer terminal.

"I know who he is! You need to focus on the costumer who's walking in through the front entrance, not the ones flying in on helicopters. Do I make myself clear?"

"Yes Sir." Bill said as Mr. Quick walked away and shook his head. Bill just threw up his shoulders expressing that he didn't know what was wrong with him.

* * * *

"They were very heavily armed!" James expressed to Cin.

"Yeah, that just how they exited the helicopters. They won't be carrying that big stuff in the Casino, but they will be armed.

"What do you think was in that trunk?" James asked curiously.

"Money, clothes, jewelry, who knows!" Cin said as another helicopter was flying in. News helicopters were lingering around trying to film from afar. The helicopter landed and the Japanese Prime Minister got off with two of is bodyguards.

Mr. Kerr and Ms. Woe another one of the Casino concierge walked over and Ms. Woe started speaking Japanese as she introduced Mr. Kerr and welcomed the Prime Minister and his two bodyguards to their suite.

Ms. Tabae came walking back and Mr. Cin said "Wow that was quick!"

"Yeah, he was tired from the flight and wanted to get some rest before the big event." Ms. Tabae said as she smiled at James and walked back over to where Mr. Kerr was standing.

Cin said "I don't know if I'm trippin or what, but I swear she just went out of her way to smile at you."

James started laughing and said "Yeah right, you're seeing things. She's way out of my league."

"You never know, but you better be careful, because Mr. Faller has been on her trail for the longest and you don't need that kind of enemy right now." Cin said as he laughed and shook his head.

"Are they missing around?" James asked.

"I don't think so, but he's after her like a hunter after its prey." Cin joked.

"Man fuck Mr. Faller, he doesn't like me anyway." James said.

"Yeah but he doesn't hate you yet either!" Cin said with a serious look on his face.

"I feel you man."

"Don't trip James, we got some of the finest women in the world that work as our show girls. You must haven't been down to the second theatre."

"I went down there once, but the janitors were the only ones there."

"Man, you're missing out on one of the hottest shows on earth. Ass everywhere and all of them is super model bad, I swear!"

"Well I'm gonna make sure I go stop through there." James said as they both smiled. They saw the President of the United State's helicopter flying up as two fighter Jets flew above it. "Now that's a boss entrance."

James said as Cin shook his head. The helicopter landed and five secret service agents got off first. It was four men and one woman agent, then the President of the United States.

"There he goes, the big shot caller." Cin said as they laughed.

"How many Leaders are you expecting to show up for this Anti Terrorism International Peace Union" James asked.

"Well we got the United Kingdom Prime Minister, Israel President, Iraq Prime Minister, Germany Chancellor, Egypt Interim President, A representative from China, India, South Africa, and Afghanistan. Not to mention Japan Prime Minister and the Sheikh's nephew. So basically it's a full house." Cin said.

Ms. Tabae escorted the President into the Casino as the Secret Service followed close by.

"She's hot!" Cin said as he was staring at the female secret service agent.

"Yeah, she hot! But she's probably above your pay grade!" James joked.

"Yeah right! I make seven figures, you're the one who gots to get his game up." Cin said as he laughed and slapped James on the back.

"Damn, seven figures!"

"Now you know why I don't sleep." And they both laughed.

* * * *

By 11:00 o'clock that evening the Casino was wide open. There was ball players, celebrities, and high rollers all over the place, not including all the people who just wanted to look, shop, eat and gamble.

James walked over to the theatres and seen Mike Epps, and Kat Williams who were performing for the open house celebration, and the new stage Play called 'Scandalous' was performing in another theatre, the Gold Stallion Showgirls was making their grand appearance as well. James thought for a second then said, "What the hell," as he headed for theatre two where the showgirls were performing.

"Hey James!"

"What's up Carl, I see that you got the best security job of them all." James joked with Carl one of the other black security guards that he met the other day.

It's more work then you could imagine! I got to stand here all day and nurse a hard on." Carl said as they laughed.

"I feel you on that! I'm gonna make a round and see what all the excitement is about." James said.

"Be my guess!" Carl said with a smile on his face as he opened up the side door to the back stage.

James walked thru the door and up the stairs and it was like he walked into a high price strip club. All the ladies were half dress putting on costumes as if it was a Victoria Secret fashion show, and the costumes were very skimpy and sexy. James was standing at the entrance to the big dressing room like a kid in a candy store, his eyes were roaming and his mouth was watering as he licked his lips.

"Excuse me Sir, can I help you?" A gay White Man walked up to him and asked.

"Oh I apologize, I'm security and I was just making my rounds."

"Well if you're looking for weapons, then you come to the right place, because all of my girls is strapped. What is your name handsome?"

"James"

"Ladies say hi to the new Casino security James."

"Hi James! All the girls said as they waved and flirted."

"Hello ladies, if you have any problems then don't hesitate to call. I'm not hard to find." James said as they all laughed and the ladies made sexy comments.

"That was cute!" The gay man said. "Well my name is Joey and I got a show to run, so please excuse us. Come on girls we got 5 minutes till curtain. This is our big debut and I need perfection. Jump to it! Joey said as he walked away.

"Bye James." A white and a Asian girl said as they both walked by.

"James if you're not busy tonight. My last show is at twelve mid night, so I'll be off at around 12:45, if you like, we can have a drink. If so come and see me, my name is Vicky." The beautiful blonde haired green eyed white girl with the playboy bunny body said.

"How can I resist!" James said as they smiled at one another and she walked off switching in her high heels and sexy costume with her perfect fat ass hanging out. "Yes I'm gonna love this job." James said to himself as he walked back out the side door.

As he went out Carl said. "You see what I mean?"

"Yes, that gotta' be torture!" James said as they both laughed and he walked away.

James went back toward the lower basement area, and as he was about to walk into the door that lead to the lower basement, Mr. Faller along with three of his gold handkerchief security guards walked out as they exited the big door. Two of the gold handkerchief security guards had big black empty sports bags.

"What are you doing down here Mr. Pryor?" Mr. Faller yelled in a hostile voice.

"I was just doing my rounds Sir!" James said.

"Well this part is off limits to you, this area is for the gold handkerchief security only. Do you understand?" Mr. Faller asked.

"Yes Sir!" James said as his jaws tightened up.

"Good, now go help the other security keep an eye on the gambling activities."

James shook his head and walked off.

James went back up to the lobby and seen Debbie and walked over to her and said, "Hey Debbie, how's everything going?"

"It's getting very interesting." She said with a smile.

"You need me to help you with anything?"

"Not at the moment, but if I need you, then I'll make sure to call you o'kay?"

"Please do!" James said as he smiled and walked away and Debbie blushed and shook her head.

Two customers were arguing with the Black Jack dealer as James walked over to see what the problem was.

"Gentlemen, Gentlemen, what's the problem?" James asked as two old black men were standing at the table.

"I told her that I didn't need a hit and she hit me anyway. I got 16 and she got a 3 showing, so why would I take a hit? He got a 4 showing and he wanted the hit not me. The hit was a 7 which busted me but would've given him 21! But since she made the mistake it messed both of our hands up." One man said.

"O'kay, I'll tell you what! Give him the 7, now dealer play the hand out." James ordered. The dealer turned over a queen of diamond and busted the house. The dealer looked up at James and James said "pay the players!" And she gave them both a $50 dollar chip. James smiled and said "good luck gentlemen," and walked away.

"Thank you," one of the players said.

James looked over at the dice table and it was packed and on the other side two slot machines went off at the same time and everyone around the machine started cheering and clapping. James looked at his watch and it was 12:15 noon so he went to the staff lounge and ordered a hamburger and fries with a cherry soda, and grabbed a empty table.

"Mind if I join you?" A cute black lady asked as she stood next to his table.

"No, by all means, have a seat! Your name is Robin right?" James asked her as he remembered that he met her at the security meeting that they attended yesterday.

"Yes, so you remembered my name?"

"Of course, I'm pretty good with names, plus it's on your name tag." James said as she looked down and started laughing.

"So how is your first day going?" Robin asked.

"I'm having the time of my life."

"Really?"

"Yes, this got to be one of the greatest jobs in the world!" I can't believe that they're paying me to do this." James said as they laughed.

"Well, that's good to hear! It is rather exciting all these rich people, stars, and celebrities all in one place. I use to only see these people on TV, now I know the meaning of acting, because some of these celebrities are a hand full." Robin joked.

"Yeah they say that money could change you." James said as they laughed and Big Ace pulled up a chair and sat down at the table.

"Hey what's up Detective Pryor? You know I was watching the news and they said that the young Black Man that you whooped was suing the Police Department for 50 million dollars. He came up on that ass whooping huh? Did you know that Detective Pryor here was the officer who whooped that young brother on TV last week?" Big Ace said as he looked at Robin.

"I better go." Robin said as she picked up her soda and walked away.

"Damn, I didn't mean to run off the cute sista. But it's only right that she knows the type of person you are," Big Ace said.

"Well while we're at it, why don't we just post your criminal record around here too! The gang that you're affiliated with, along with robbery and drug charge that you got! My good friend is on the Executive Staff here at the Casino, that's how I got this job, and I bet that I can easily have you fired if I ask."

"Wait a minute man; I'm just joking with you. You know I'm just riding you for putting me in prison, that's all." Big Ace said nervously.

"Look here John or Big Ace, whatever you call yourself these days. If you ever disrespect me like that again, I'll have your ass fired, then I'll have my good friends down at the Police Station be on you like flies on shit!"

"Man we ain't got to go there, we cool." Big Ace said as he got up and walked out.

James finished the rest of his food then left.

Chapter 5

It was later on that day at 5:10 p.m. and the Casino was packed. Everyone showed up for their reservations and the President was scheduled to have his Anti-Terrorism International Peace Union meeting at 6 o'clock. All of the political representatives were walking around mingling with the people with their bodyguards surrounding them, as if they were campaigning. Big money was being spent, and all of the gambling tables were being occupied.

James walked over to Cin and Mr. Adam White and said, "It looks like Gold Stallion is a big hit!"

"Yes it is Mr. Pryor, I was just sharing the same sentiments with Mr. Cin., Mr. Adam White said with a joyful smile.

"Are you enjoying your first day Mr. Pryor?"

"Yes, by all means Sir, and I'm grateful for the opportunity to work for you," James added.

"You're a good worker, just do your job and stay out of trouble, and it's here for you to enjoy." Mr. Adam White said as he patted James on the back and walked away.

"He's a cool dude!" James said to Cin.

"Yes, very good man! But he doesn't care for Mr. Faller and Mr. Quick and their security crew. They tried to get him fired, but my uncle likes him too much." Cin laughed.

"Well, he's not alone because I don't care for them either. I ran into Mr. Faller and a few of his security crew when I was doing rounds down by the second bottom basement floor, and he got mad at me and told me that I couldn't be down there." James said.

"He's a liar, you got clearance to go anywhere in this Casino, he was just trying to get under your skin to see if you'll snap, so he can have something on you. Don't mind him, do your job and if he asks, tell him that I sent you." Cin said.

"Ain't he your boss too?" James asked.

"Yes and No! I'm the big boss nephew, so he can't really tell me shit. I report to my uncle if I want too!"

"That's what seven figures get you?" James joked.

"You damn right, and being his sister's only child doesn't hurt either!" And they both started laughing.

"Do your rounds and I'll catch up with you later! I got to make sure that the ballroom is ready for the President."

"O'kay, see you later!" James said as they departed. James really liked Cin, he's a cool well grounded young man. James reached the elevator and a Bell Boy walked up to him.

"Hey James, I've been looking all over for you. Ms. Birch wanted to see you on the twentieth floor room 502!"

"Thank you Alex." James said.

"No problem." Alex said as James step into the elevator and told old man Joe the twentieth floor.

"Twentieth floor it is." Joe said.

James walked up to the door and gently knocked and her bodyguard answered. "Ms. Birch requested to see me?" James said to the big bodyguard.

"Yes Mr. James, she's in the other room waiting for you." The bodyguard replied as James walked in toward the bedroom and the bodyguard extended his arm directing James toward the bedroom suite.

James walked to the bedroom suite door and gentle knocked on it. "Come in." A soft voice uttered from the bedroom.

James opened up the door and Ms. Birch was standing there in a silk peach robe. "Come in James, I'm not gonna bite." She said as she grabbed his arm and gently pulled him into the bedroom and closed the door.

"Excuse me Miss, the Bell Boy said that you wanted to see me?" James said with a curious look on his face.

"Yes James, I wanted to give you something."

"And what might that be?" James asked!

"This!" And she opened up her silk robe and was completely naked underneath.

"Wow umm! That's nice, but that's not in my job description." James said nervously as he gazed at her sexy figure.

"Nobody will have to know." She said as she walked toward him and he began walking backwards, then she pinned him up against the wall.

"Listen Ms. Birch, you are a very beautiful lady, but I'll lose my job for this!" James said as she was caressing his body through his clothes.

James kept his hand on the butt of his 45 Automatic to secure it. She rubbed his arm down to his hand and felt his gun and said. "Wow you got a big gun, I love a man with a big gun, then grabbed his dick through his pants and noticed that he was rock hard. "Someone wants to play!" She said and laughed as James tried to pull away and she pushed him back on the wall and started to kiss him.

"Wait, wait Ms. Birch."

"Call me Eve!"

"Eve, I'll lose my job for this!" James said as he nudged her back some.

"James, you will lose your job if I told them that you tried to sexually assault me."

"You wouldn't do that!"

"Do you want to try me?" James looked into her eyes and seen lust, and knew that this crazy woman would probably do something crazy like that if he didn't give her what she wanted.

She started undressing him and kissing him some more on the neck, face and lips. "What about your bodyguard?"

"What about him?" She said as they laughed and James put his gun on the side dresser and started kicking off his shoes and taking off his shirt and boxers.

She giggled and pulled out a condom from the dresser drawers and grabbed James dick and started sucking it as she sat on the edge of the bed and he stood over her. "You like that?"

"Hell yeah!" James said as his toes curled.

She slid the condom over his dick and pulled him up on the bed as he slid between her body and started licking on her sexy pussy lips. Her back arched as he slid his tongue deep into her pussy, and she let out a sexy moan. James licked up her body and started sucking her full breast as he slid his dick deep off into her pussy. She moaned louder as James started to fuck her slow and deep. She met his hump with each thrust as they fucked in harmony. James kissed her to try and muffle her moans, then flipped her over and pulled her hips back to him as he slid into her wet pussy, and grabbed her by her long blonde hair and pulled it back hard as she let out a low scream and James started fucking her hard and fast from the back. She was moaning loud and saying "I'm coming, I'm coming oooowow!" She screamed as they both came together.

James fell on top of her as they both started laughing. "That was good!" James whispered into her ear as they kissed and he rolled off of her.

"Yes, you are an animal James!" Eve said as she pulled the condom off his dick, and went to the bathroom and flushed it down the toilet. Then came back out with a warm wet washcloth and cleaned his dick off. She started smiling at him and said, "That was a pretty good performance, but now it's my turn." And went down and started sucking his dick again.

James looked down at her and made a look of surprise as he laid back and let her do her thing. Two minute later he was back fully hard, and she placed another condom on his dick and straddled him as she guided his dick into her hot wet pussy and started riding him like a porno star. Twenty minutes later they came together again and cuddled up as they both dozed off.

* * * *

The Sheikh's nephew was in his suite with 20 of his most trusted colleagues.

"Gentlemen, this is the day that we make history. Is our brothers in position." The Sheikh's nephew said.

"Yes Sir, they're just awaiting for your order." His right hand man said.

"Good, about this time tomorrow we all will be very wealthy men." The Sheikh's nephew said as he put the clip in his Mac 11 and put his 9mm in his belt with 4 extra clips in his pockets. "A toast to success!" Everyone held up there glasses and downed the expensive liquor.

* * * *

The President's meeting was taken place and Ted, Bill and five other computer specialists was watching it on the big TV monitor. "This is a historical event here." Ted said.

"So is that tuna sandwich that I ate a couple hours ago, because it's fighting to come out." Bill said as he grabbed his stomach and headed to the restroom.

"Look over there the Sheikh's nephew is finally coming out of his suite, and he has about 20 armed guards with big machine guns. They ain't supposed to have machine guns in the Casino. Mike said as the phone rang.

"Yes, Gold Stallion security how may I help you? Who did you say you where? The Saudi Arabian investigation department? He don't? Yes! O'kay, will call you back soon." (Click)

"The Saudi Arabian Sheikh do not have a nephew here. He's a impostor! Radio Mr. Quick, hurry." Ted yelled to Suzy, then ran in the restroom to tell Bill. "Bill, Bill!" Ted yelled.

"What? Can't you see that I'm busy." Bill said from inside one of the stalls.

"The Sheikh's nephew is a fraud! We just got a call from the Saudi Arabian investigation department, and they said that the Sheikh doesn't have a nephew here.

"Call Mr. Quick and place a Code Red over the radio to the Security Team!"

"Got you!"

* * * *

As Ted ran into the bathroom to tell Bill the news. Two Gold Handkerchief Security Guards walked into the computer room and Mike said. "We're glad that you guys are here. We just got the call from Saudi Arabia that the Sheikh's nephew is an impostor, and they're heavily armed entering the elevator and stairwell."

"Did you call anyone?"

"We were about to," Suzy said as she picked up the two-way radio and both of the securities pulled out their guns with silencer attachments and started shooting everyone in the room.

Ted said, "What the hell," as he heard the scream and noise coming from the computer room and he opened up the restroom door, and was shot three times as he fell back into the restroom dead.

"Oh shit!" Bill whispered as he pulled up his pants and stepped on top of the toilet.

The door busted open and the Gold Handkerchief guards shot Ted again in the forehead, then looked under the stall doors and said, "It's clear! He must've finish taking a shit, because he got that whole restroom stinking." And shut the restroom door back as they laughed.

The other one jumped on the radio and said "Security Team two got eyes on the prize, over.

"Copy!" A voice said over the radio.

"Security Team one is on the move." The Sheikh's nephew right hand man said. As they got off the elevator on the ballroom floor two secret service agents was at the ballroom door with two of Israel President's bodyguards, and they notices the Sheikh's nephew with ten bodyguards coming toward them and before they knew it, eight silent shots rung through the air and killed them dead. The double doors swung open and the Sheikh's nephew ten men crew began shooting every security guard that was standing around. Everyone in the room was caught off guard as the bullets rang out in silence. Two guards pulled their weapons but shot in vain, as bullets ate up their bodies. When the smoke cleared, the Leaders body guards was laid out slain on the bloody carpet.

"What is the meaning of this murderous outrage?" The President of the United State's yelled.

The Sheikh's nephew grabbed the President off the podium and socked him in the face, then threw him down off the stage unto the ground. "I am Abby Shakur and this

71

is a Terrorist Act, if you do anything stupid you will die! If you do not do as we say, you will die! We have taken the whole Casino hostage, so if you do not comply with our request, then a lot of innocent people will die. Now my comrades will relieve you of your phones and electronic devices, and any weapons that you may have."

"We have no quarms with Saudi Arabia, why are you wedging war on the United States?" The President asked.

"Who said that we are Saudi Arabians." Abby said as he laughed. His comrades were taking all of the guns and electronic devices off the Leaders and the dead bodyguards.

* * * *

James heard two loud whispers and a hard bang against the floor as he jumped up quick, and grabbed his 45 automatic off the side table and went and ducked into the bathroom doorway and cut off the lights. Eve looked up from here sleepy state and said, "what's wrong baby?" As the door got kicked opened and she screamed as the man with an Kaffiyeh head garb and his face covered up aimed his gun.

James said, "FREEZE!" And the man tried to turn towards James with his gun, and James shot him three times and dropped him dead.

James went over and removed the gun that had a silencer on it, then pulled the Kaffiyeh up over the man's face and said "Ed!"

"Who's Ed, and why did he try to kill us?" Eve said.

"I don't know" James said as he look out of the bedroom door into the living room suite, and seen her bodyguard lying dead on the rug. "Damn, get dress quick!" James yelled as he rushed to put on his clothes.

"Where's Freddy?" Eve asked. Who?

"Freddy my bodyguard!"

"He's dead!"

"Dead? She asked as she slid on her Versace dress and boots.

"Yeah!" James said as she ran out the door to the dead bodyguard. "Wait! silly girl." James said as he put on his suit jacket and heard Eve scream as he peeped out, and seen another man standing over her with his gun aimed at her head. James came out of the room bustin his 45 automatic as he was walking up, and the man's blood splatter all over the back wall as he fell over Eve.

Eve pushed the man off her as she jumped up with blood on her dress and arm. "Who are they?"

"I don't know but we got to go.....come on!"

"I got to get this blood off of me first," Eve said.

"It's gonna be your blood if you don't come on." James said as he reached down and grabbed the extra clips that the dead man had on him and his gun and military two-way radio.

James peaked outside of the door of the suite, and saw that the door across from them was open, so he grabbed Eve and they ran across to the other suite. A dead man and two women were laying dead on the floor. James picked up the phone but there was no deal tone. Then he heard a voice come over the military two-way radio "The cabinet is secure we have the Leaders, go to faze three!"

"Copy that!" Another voice said.

"Eve, Eve where are you?" James whispered loud.

"I'm here! I had to wipe that blood off me. It had me feeling icky!" Eve said as she made a nasty face.

"Listen girl, something big is going down here, and it's real bad, so stays closes and keep your eyes open o'kay!"

"O'kay" Eve said as James ran over to the big picture window and saw people running like crazy.

"Damn come on!" James said.

* * * *

Fifteen mask men ran into the gambling part of the Casino, and started shooting the arm guards, everyone in the Casino started running out the front door. "What is the meaning of this Mr. Adam White the executive security manager said, as he held up his hands and approached one of the gun men.

Mr. White recognized a familiar look in the gun man's eyes!

"It's you!" He said, the gun man just smiled and opened fire on Mr. White killing him dead.

An elderly man and lady was sitting at the Black Jack table with the dealer, and a mask man shouted, "Get out of here, NOW! Then he shot his AR-15 in the air, the elderly couple jumped-up and started running out while the dealer held onto their arms helping them so they wouldn't fall.

Eighty percent of the people ran out the doors as the mask man grabbed his military two-way radio and order, "Close and seal the doors!"

"Copy that!" A voice replied over the radio as the bullet proof doors locked and a gated steel-bar rolled between the doors to secure them.

"Doors are secure!"

Carl was watching the back door to the Showgirls dressing room, standing inside trying to sneak a peek of the Showgirls as they got dressed for their next performance. Suddenly the back door opened up and four masked men walked in, one of them shot Carl in the face, blowing his brains out the back side of his head.

"AAAH! All the women started screaming as one of the mask men shouted, "Shut up, shut up before you be next!" The women got quiet. "Now that's better, you got one minute to get dress, then come and form a line right here. Hurry up now! O'kay, I need all of you to follow my friend there, and if anyone is hiding then you all will be shot and killed."

Joey the gay Showgirls Choreographer ran out and cried, "please don't shoot us, we're just performers."

"Shut up, and fall in line! Is anyone else back there? O'kay move out!" The Leader of the mask men looked at one of his comrades and said, "sweep this place, if anyone is hiding kill'em!"

"O'kay boss" The mask man said as he did his sweep.

When the four mask men entered the back door, five other ones went thru the front entrance, and held everyone in the theatre at gun point. Other performers and customers were being escorted from the two other theatres, until the place was packed. The masked men went around and searched all of the people taking their phones and electronic devices off of them.

"Listen up everyone," the Leader shot in the air and got everyone's attention as he stood on stage. "We are a Terrorist organization, and we have seized this entire Casino. As long as you do everything we say, we'll not harm you, but if you try anything stupid, then we'll kill you. Sit tight and we will be out of your way in a few hours." The Leader looked at five of his heavily armed men, two was stationed on the stage, and three spread out over the theatre, they raised their hand, as the Leader and twenty of his followers walked out the front doors.

* * * *

The President Secret Service Agent Yvonne was doing her rounds, and as she walked up the stairwell to the

10th floor, and got to the computer room she saw everyone shot dead on the floor except two mask men who were operating the computer controls terminal. She watched and on the computer monitor she saw the ballroom were the President and the Leaders were being held at gun point, and on the small screen monitor in the corner of the room it showed the game room lobby being emptied by other mask men. As she watched and listened, she heard a voice come over the radio saying, "close and seal the doors!"

The mask man at the control terminal replied, "Copy That!" Then he pushed a button and confirmed, "Doors Closed!"

Yvonne clenched her 9mm and walked thru the opened glass door and order, "Put your damn hands up!" The two mask men looked at her then at each other, and went for their guns. She unloaded two shots in the first man hitting him in the forehead and throat, then shot the second man three times twice in the bullet proof vest and once in the face. The second man laid on the floor in shock as Yvonne walked up on him and kicked his gun away. She looked at his wound and saw that one bullet went thru his bullet proof vest and hit his lungs because he was gagging for breath. "What is going on? Why are you in here killing innocent people?"

He laughed and coughed up some blood and whispered, "You all are going to die!" And laughed some more as he coughed again then died.

The bathroom door cracked open as Yvonne swung her gun around at the door. "Don't shoot, don't shoot!" Bill said as he peeped out.

"Open-up the door slowly and keep your hands where I can see them" Yvonne ordered as Bill came out of the restroom.

"I work here, I'm the computer specialist! I think I know what's going on." Bill said as he looked around at his co-worker laying dead on the floor. "Oh this is terrible."

"Tell me what's going on?" Yvonne said as she picked up both the dead men guns and extra clips, then grabbed the Tec 9 that was on the empty chair.

"Well, Ted told me before he died, that an investigator from Saudi Arabia called, and said that the Sheikh didn't have a nephew out here at this Casino. I guess the news must've reported it. See that's him in the Ballroom with the President!. Look they took over the theatre and headed for the retail shops and restaurants. They're all over the place, and the police is everywhere outside. But the front doors are locked and the security bar is closed!" Bill said.

"Can you open the doors?" Yvonne asked.

"Of course!" Bill said as he went over to the computer controls and opened back up the security doors.

A mask man that was posted up in the lobby by the slot machines saw the security gates open and jumped on his radio and said Team One, the security gates to the front passage just opened, Team Six out!

"Copy that Team Six, are you sure?"

"Yes sir, I'm very sure!"

"O'kay hold your position and use deadly force if necessary, assistance is on the way!"

"Team Two do you copy?" A voice was coming over the military radio as Yvonne and Bill listened.

"Here they come," Bill said as he seen ten mask men running toward the elevator and four of the ten ran up the stairwell. "Let's go" Yvonne said as Bill grabbed his coat and Yvonne turned toward the big computer system and unloaded a clip from the Tec-9 into the monitors and control system. Then they ran out as Yvonne reloaded the Tec-9 and ran for the stairwell.

The mask men were on the fourth floor climbing fast as Yvonne and Bill started running up the stairs to the upper floors. The mask men heard them running on the upper stairs and called out over the military radio "Team Five they're headed to the upper floors."

"Copy!" The mask men on the elevator said, as three got off on the 12th floor to secure the computer room, and the other ones rode the elevator to the nineteenth floor and got off and ran into the stairwell to cut the suspects off.

Yvonne heard the upper stairwell door open, and knew that they were right above her, so she waited on the eighteenth floor and as they tried to creep down the stairs she started blastin them with her Tec-9. She killed the first man as he tumbled down the stairs, and the other two started exchanging fire with her. The four men that were running up the stairs were still climbing but they slowed down as fatigue started setting in.

James heard the call come over the radio right before him and Eve hit the stairwell. He held his finger up to his lips telling Eve to be quiet as they crept onto the twentieth floor stairwell, and started creeping down. He saw the two mask men shooting down the stairs and said, "Hey!" And as they turned and looked, he shot them both in the head. He then grabbed their guns and said, "It's clear now," as two bodies fell down from the upper stairwell.

"Identify yourself!" A voice hollered out.

"I'm Casino Security my name is, "James Pryor.""

"James is that you?"

"Who is that?"

"It's Bill!"

"Computer Specialist?" James shouted back.

"Yes that him, come on!" Bill said as he raced up the stairs and Yvonne slowly approached with her gun aimed at him.

"Hold down little momma, I'm on your side!" James said.

"How do I know that?" Yvonne asked.

"Well if the two bodies aren't enough, then it's two more upstairs. You're that Secret Service agent huh?"

"How do you know that?" Yvonne asked

"Because, I seen you and four other agents get off the helicopter with the President earlier today," James replied.

"Team Five confirm, Team Five confirm over!" A voice came over the military radio.

"Well I don't have time for this, you can come with me or you can stay here, it's your choice!" James said as he walked back down to the nineteenth floor passed the dead bodies and onto the elevator. Old man Joe was slumped in the corner of the elevator dead. James pulled him out and sat him up against the wall, and jumped on the elevator.

"James where are you going they're everywhere." Yvonne said as Bill shook his head in agreement.

"Well the way I see it, once they find these dead bodies then they're gonna be sweeping the upstairs floors looking for us, so we better try to make it down before they make it up."

Everyone jumped on the elevator as James push the second floor. He changed the clip in AR-15 that he just took off the mask gunman and said, "If this elevator should stop at any other floor before we reach the second floor, then shoot to kill," and handed Bill and Eve a 9mm each.

The elevator went all the way to the second floor without stopping. James got off with his AR-15 rifle aimed to shoot. He looked around then signaled for them to get off. Then he pushed the button to the twenty- fourth floor on the elevator and sent it back up. They walked down the hallway and seen that most of the doors were cracked. A few dead bodies laid face down in blood in few of the rooms, so they closed the doors. "I don't know what's going on but it's big!" James said as he looked out of the window at all the cop cars and lights.

"They took over the Ballroom and seized the President and all of the Leaders." Yvonne said.

"I kind of figured that, but if they're alive, then it's for a reason." James said as he analyzed the situation.

"They took over the theatres and everything. They put everyone in theatre two, with five armed guards watching them." Bill said.

"How do you know that?" James questioned.

"Because we saw them on the computer system," Bill replied.

"We also unlocked the front doors and took the security off, so the police can have access. Then we destroyed the computer system." Yvonne said with a smile.

"Good for you guys, now that will buy us some time," James said.

"What are we gonna do?" Yvonne asked.

"It's either us or them, so we kill as many as we can, in hopes that the police make it here on time." James said.

"I have to save the President!" Yvonne said.

"We will, but first let's try to even the odds!" James said as he thought about Janet and clinched his gun. "Get ready we leave in ten minutes."

Chapter 6

Abby Shakur stood on the podium with his Kaffiyah on covering his face, and some dark sunglasses while his right hand man filmed him and posted it live on Youtube. "We are an Independent Terrorist Organization who has seized control over your fellow Leaders." Then he read off all the Leader's names and countries where they are from, and the camera slowly canvesed the room viewing each member sitting in his chair at the table while Abby's men were standing behind them with machine guns pointed at their heads. "We request the following...! One billion dollars for each member released safely, within three hours, or we will start killing them one by one, live over Internet every five minutes until our demands are met. The banks that you will deposit this money in will be the following banks, and your conformation number and code will be sent to this number. If any attempts to rescue these Leaders, we will kill one and attack back with destruction as demonstrated here. He picked up his I-phone and made a call and 30 seconds later two car bombs exploded at the local Police Station blowing up a quarter of the building. He hung up the I-phone and said, "That was just a small illustration. You got three hours." The video picture went dead.

* * * *

James and them was watching the video on the TV News Station, and when the Police Station exploded James said, "it just got personal!"

"These are professional Terrorist!" Eve screamed.

"Yes, this was well planned out. Remembered those men that I killed in your suite? James asked Eve.

"Yes!"

"Well, one of them worked security in this building. He was considered one of the elite security guard's on the Gold Handkerchief Team. Which was ran by Mr. Faller the Executive Security Manager. He, Mr. Cin, Mr. Quick, and Mr. White ran the security detail. Now I suspect Mr. Faller and Mr. Quick is involved with this Terrorist scheme, but I can't eliminate Mr. Cin and Mr. White yet. However, they had around 25 employees that work here that I believe is involved, not including the ones who were probably a Bell Boy, or perhaps some other job description. So we can't trust no one James insisted.

"Wow that really put the odds against us." Eve said.

"Well we better be safe than sorry!" Bill remarked as he downed the small complimentary bottle of Brandy.

"Come on, we got to move!" James said.

"Wait! What if you start killing them off, and they start killing the Leaders?" Eve argued.

"Well, in the position we're in, we're already considered dead, and they are too, because these Terrorist are blood thirsty maniacs, and right now we have no choice, either kill or be killed." Yvonne lectured.

"O'kay, now that we're on the same page, let's go cause havoc!" James said.

* * * *

"Janet! Hi babe are you o'kay?" Debbie said as she gave Janet a hug in the theatre.

"Yes, I'm fine! What is going on Janet asked?

"I don't know!   But, I think that Terrorist have taken over the Ballroom and are holding the President and Leaders hostage. They've already killed a lot of innocent people for nothing," Debbie said.

"Have you seen James?" Janet asked with a concerned look on her face.

"No I haven't, but he might be held in another area."

"I hope so!" Janet said as her eyes swelled up with tears and Debbie gave her a hugged.

* * * *

Police from every department was outside, the local police, FBI, Secret Service, and SWAT. The whole scene was chaotic. The Captain of the Police Department was in a rage arguing with other top officials. "Listen, those crazy bastards just blew up my damn Police Station. I want my SWAT Team in on the raid!"

"Listen Captain Fields, this is a Government matter, the FBI has jurisdiction here!"

"Well I hate to intervene into you guys little debate, but the President of the United States is in there, so it's a Secret Service issue."

An Army vehicle pulled up and a Four Star General stepped out and proceeded to walk over to where the department head was debating on who was in charge.

"Excuse me gentlemen, who's in charge here!" The General asked.

"I am! My name is Mr. Web!"

I must inform you that this is now United States Army jurisdiction via the Vice President's authorization. Casualties such as this regarding the President's capture call for an executive transfer of power, the Vice President has just been sworn into oath, by the Executive Chief of Staff. I won't bore you with statutes, but I have been giving orders by the Vice President to oversee this Terrorist Plot. As you know the United States do not negotiate with Terrorist. Therefore, my Special Force Team is preparing to enter the building from the roof as another Team is assembling to make preparations to create a diversion thru the front entrance," the General ordered!

"That would be impossible considering that the Casino is equipped with bullet proof glass and thick steel gates." Captain Fields replied.

"That shouldn't be a problem because we got conformation that the front door security system has been removed five minutes ago. Plus, it's only a brief diversion unless it's successful." General Hart stated as he picked up his military two-way radio and said, "It's a go!"

The Combat Team stormed the front entrance using mild explosive as an army helicopter flew toward the Casino.

* * * *

"Sir, we got an armed Team moving in toward the front entrance." One of the Terrorist said into his military radio.

"Team Four, you know what to do!" A voice replied thru the radio.

"Copy?" Team Four, Leader said as he grabbed his electronic device, "On my lord!"

"What is it Team Four Leader?"

"Sir, we got a birdie in the sky carrying hostiles!"

"O'kay Team Seven, you know what to do!"

"Copy!"

The Assault Team blew the first door and ran into the foyer toward the next bullet proof door. And one Assault Team member shouted, "Explosive, Explosive!" (Boom) A small bomb went off and killed nine out of the fifteen Assault Members.

The second bullet proof doors opened and five members of the Terrorist Team rushed out with ski mask on and started shooting the other Assault Team Members who were injured and in a daze from the blast. One Terrorist member ran to the outside entrance and fired a rocket launcher blowing up a SWAT truck that was blocking the entrance of the Casino. The police that were outside started exchanging fire killing one Terrorist and injuring another, the rest of the Terrorist group retreated back into the Casino.

The helicopter was closing in as two Terrorist ran out with rocket launchers and shot at the helicopter. The first rocket missed, but the second one hit the back end of the helicopter causing it to spin out of control, as two Seal Members fell out of the helicopter and the helicopter crashed into the golf course. Then two Terrorist lend over the Casino building and fired two more rocket launchers at the crowd of police, and two vehicles exploded killing and wounding all the police around them.

"Where are the Paramedics? Help these officers now! Officer Burk get your SWAT Team sharp shooters aiming at the roof, and shoot anyone who looks over, THAT'S AN ORDER!" Captain Fields yelled.

"Captain this is still my jurisdiction!" The General hollered.

"Not anymore and if you don't like it, then arrest me!" The captain yelled as he went to go attend to his officers.

* * * *

Big Ace and Sammy was on the twenty-third floor going from suite to suite getting their loot on.

"Big Ace look at this diamond necklace and the matching bracelet, and earrings that was there too. This got to be worth a couple hundred g's!" Sammy said.

"Listen, don't forget that we're splitting everything 50/50." Big Ace reminded Sammy.

"I know, and I seen you take that diamond Rolex off that dead man too! Don't think I didn't see that fool!" Sammy joked.

"Man I wasn't trying to hide it... I'm gonna check the other room! Big Ace said as he walked off.

"O'kay, hey I found the stash!" Damn this got to be at least 20g's in hundred dollar bills." Sammy said to himself, as he turned around right into a barrel of an AR-15 and a short stocky built Terrorist was standing there with a ski mask on."

If this is your money man, you can have it back, I ain't trippin. Come on man don't kill me, I got a little boy and a little girl, man. I don't care about this Terrorist shit ya'll on. Come on man!" Sammy begged as the Terrorist brung the AR-15 rifle up to Sammy's head. Sammy ducked down real fast as Big Ace hit the Terrorist over the head with a gold brass lamp and the Terrorist shot a bullet out the AR-15 rifle with the silencer that hit the wall. The Terrorist fell to the ground, and Big Ace started socking him in the face as he snatched the AR-15 from the Terrorist hand, then Sammy started kicking the Terrorist and stomping his face.

"Get the other gun man, damn get the other fucking gun man!" Big Ace shouted as Sammy reach down and grabbed the big 40 gloc and the extra clips and the Military radio off his belt, and handed Big Ace the two AR-15 clips, then looked back at the Terrorist and started stomping him some more.

"Don't you ever pull a gun on another Black Man! Can I kill him?" Sammy asked.

"It's a violation of your parole!"

"But he is a Terrorist! See who he is." Big Ace said as Sammy pulled off his ski mask. Damn, that looks like Joe the gold handkerchief security guard."

"Look like, that's Joe punk ass." Sammy said as he started to kick Joe some more and said, "I never liked your punk ass anyway."

"What, What? Did he see you take anything?" Big Ace asked.

"Yeah, this money!" Sammy said as he pulled out a wad of hundreds dollar bills.

"Well you might need to shoot him, he seen too much, and might tell on us if we let him go.

"You're right!" (Pow) Sammy shot him.

"That was gangsta! Let's roll." Big Ace said as they walked out and when they turned in the hallway two more Terrorists was coming out of another suite. They froze, as Big Ace and Sammy started shooting at the Terrorist who were caught off guard and tried to shoot back, but they were to late as there bullets hit the wall and ceiling as Big Ace and Sammy unloaded on them.

"We got them, we got them!" Sammy hollered with excitement.

"Go grab their guns and ammo so we can get out of here. I'll watch your back!" Big Ace said as Sammy ran over and grabbed the other AR-15 rifle two 45 automatics and seven extra clips.

"Should I take their bullet proof vest off?" Sammy asked.

"It doesn't look like it worked for them!" Big Ace said.

"You're right!" Sammy said as they ran to the stairwell and eased down. They heard a loud explosion and the Casino walls shook. "Oh shit, what's that?"

"I don't know, but we need to make it to the lower floors before this muthafucka cave in. Come on!" Big Ace said as they rushed down a bit faster.

* * * *

James, Eve, Bill and Yvonne was creeping thru the Casino on the lobby floor, when they seen all hell break loose. The Assault Team tried to penetrate the front entrance while twenty mask Terrorist was stationed in different locations. James and them squatted down behind the check in counter, across from the lobby and they peeped around the counter when all hell broke loose. A loud explosion occurred, as the Terrorist began to advanced on the entrance way. James seen that all of the attention was diverted toward the entrance so he whispered "We got to move out now! Go around that way to the restaurant and I'll cover you."

"O'kay come on" Yvonne said as she lead the way.

"One Terrorist was behind a slot machine twenty yards away and saw Yvonne, Bill, and Eve run from the counter around the corner, and when he turn to look back at the counter James shot him dead with the AR-15 rifle with the silencer on. James saw another one ducked down by the Black Jack table, and shot him too. Then ran around the corner and peeped back out and shot another masked Terrorist that was advancing from the back. James heard Yvonne whisper for him to come on, and he ran to catch up with them.

They crept thru the kitchen down the back steps to the basement where Janet worked, and her office was empty. "Janet! Janet!" James whispered then said "Damn!"

"Who is Janet?" Yvonne asked.

"She's my sister."

"Don't worry we'll find her, she's probably in the theatre with the rest of the hostages." Yvonne said.

"We got to go rescue them!" James said.

"Even if we do, where are we gonna take them to?" Yvonne asked.

"Did you say that you disabled the entrance doors?" James asked.

"Yes"

"Well we need to create a diversion so we can lure the majority of the Terrorist away from the front entrance, so we can take out the rest, and lead the hostage out through the front entrance." James said.

"Sounds like a plan, but how are we gonna cause a diversion?" Bill asked.

"Someone coming this way" Yvonne whispered.

"Hide, everyone hide somewhere!" James said as everyone ducked in a hiding spot.

Three mask men walked by as James tip toed by the office door to see which way they went, "Come on, but stay on point." James whispered as he led the way out and Yvonne stayed in the rear.

James looked around the corner and seen six Terrorist surrounding a laptop computer.

"What are they doing?" Yvonne asked.

"I don't know, but we better stop them! Eve if anyone comes from the back, you shoot them o'kay!"

"O'kay"

"Come on let's do this! Bill go around the side, Yvonne shoot to kill, but don't shoot the computer!"

"No problem boss!" Yvonne said, as they walked out from around the corner taking the Terrorist by surprise, then they started unloading their AR-15 rifle into the Terrorist upper body. All six Terrorist fell to the floor shaking to their death. James and Yvonne ran over and stripped their weapons off, then Bill walked from the other side as Eve stayed by the hallway entrance, where they came in at.

"What were they doing?" James asked.

"Let me see! Bill said as he looked at the laptop computer. Oh shit, they're stealing money from all of the banks all over the world!"

"How much have they stole?" James asked.

"Right now it's at a hundred and forty two billion, six hundred and fifteen million, seven hundred and twenty thousand and eight hundred dollars." Bill said.

"Damn, that's a lot of money!" James said.

"Yeah, it's downloading a million dollars every minute!" Bill said.

"Can you stop it?" Yvonne said.

"Better than that, do you know your bank account access number?" Bill asked

"Sure!" Yvonne said.

"Where is your bank located, what the name and what's the number?

"Washington D.C., Bank of America, account #8655 332764 99651."

"What's your five digit money routing code?"

"35549!"

"How do you remember all of them numbers?" James asked.

"I've always been good with numbers!" Yvonne said.

"There you are, you are now the riches woman in the world" Bill said with a smile.

"You transfer all of that money into my account?" Yvonne asked.

"Yep, now you got the only bargaining chip" Bill said then started punching on the computer.

"What are you doing?" James asked,

"I'm trying to disconnect," Bill said.

"Grab their guns and ammo and let's see who they are! Just as I thought that's Mr. Faller's Gold Handkerchief Security Team. That means he got to be involved."

"Team Ten how much longer? Team Ten, confirm your standing?" A voice came over the radio.

"O'kay! Party's over, time to go!" James called out.

Bill punched in some keys on the computer then grabbed the thumb drive out of the USB port, then snatched the wire out of the circuit and shot the computer.

"Come on Bill!" James hollered as they ran out the back way down to the bottom basement floor were Mr. Faller told James that he didn't have authorization to go.

"Everybody stopped to catch their breath and Bill said, "their gonna be really after us now, so we better act fast."

"Oh shit, tell me that that's not what I think it is" Eve said as she pointed to two big round plastic barrels with wires and C-4 tape around it.

"It's a bomb!" Bill said in a panic.

Yvonne and James ran over to it. "They plan on blowing up the place after they downloaded all the money. The request for ransom was just a smoke screen. They was really trying to steal the money from all the banks, and they needed this high tech computer banking system to do it"

"Well, I hate to have to rain on their parade, but they have to do better than this. Because this explosive system is first grade shit!" Yvonne said as she disconnected one of the bomb's detonators and the light went off. Then she went over to the other one and did the same.

"Do you guys see anymore around here?" Everybody started looking around, "here's another one over here," Eve said.

Yvonne ran over to disconnect it.

"Watch out" Bill said as he unloaded his AR-15 rifle at two men sneaking up. One of them jumped behind a wall as two more appeared from the entrance and James gunned them down too.

The Terrorist who was behind the wall was protected from James and Bill assault, as he grabbed his military radio and said, "they're in the second basement I need assistance."

"Hold these!" Yvonne gave Eve the detonators, and cut a block of C-4 off the barrel and tossed it by the mask Terrorist feet and when he saw it, he ran from his spot trying to take cover and Yvonne picked him off, as he fell twitching on the ground.

"Come on let's go, this way quick!" James yelled as they ran down a back hallway, and around to the back of the first theatre. "Give me those," James grabbed the detonators and hid them inside a trash can in a Kentucky Fried Chicken bag. "Come on let's go!" James said as they saw two dead Casino security guards lying in a pool of blood. James shook his head and bit his jaws tight as he walked by them hoping Janet was alright.

Chapter 7

"Gentlemen I got some good news and some bad news!" Abby said as he walked back up to the podium and his right hand man had the video camera back on him as he spoke. "The good news is that, Mr. Woo government has paid the billion dollar ransom that was requested, so Mr. Woo you will be escorted out of here as I promised, and please no hard feelings. You may go in peace! Please escort Mr. Woo to the front entrance." One armed guard lead Mr. Woo out of the doors of the ballroom and "for the bad news! Since the police officers tried to enter into the Casino and disrespected my orders and authorities, then it's only right that I keep my promise and display my power." He called up two of his guards and whispers something to them and they went over to the Egyptian President and drugged him to the foot of the stage.

"Wait a minute, for god sake you don't have to do this" The President pleaded.

"Quiet, or you will be next" Abby said as he pulled out a big knife and walked over while his men was holding the Egyptian President down. Abby said, "May you sleep with the Pharaohs" and stabbed him in the heart as the world watched him shake to his death on live cable TV.

"We will not stand for anymore disrespect," and he picked up his I-phone and made a call, and 30 seconds later a car at a local gas station blew-up. "His blood is on your hands!" Abby said as the video ended.

Mr. Woo walked right out of the front door when SWAT surrounded him, then threw him on the ground handcuffed him, searched him, and drugged him to the other side away from the front entrance.

Everybody in the ballroom was watching it on the big screen TV and Abby looked at the President and said "Look, NO RESPECT! They treat a ruler like a criminal. As if he was a Black Man. NO RESPECT!" and everyone looked at the United State's President as he held his head down.

* * * *

"Look Big Ace!" Big Ace glanced in the room right before the staff lounge, and it was filled with about fifteen dead bodies.

"Damn, these muthafucka are salvages!" Big Ace said

"Ain't that little Scott?" Sammy said as he pointed to the young red head white boy that was on the bottom of the pile.

"Yup, that's him! And that's Mr. Adam White next to him. Big Ace walked over and reached in Mr. Adam white pocket.

"Man don't take his money, he was cool!" Sammy argued.

"I'm not taking his damn money. Mr. White got the keys to the city!" Big Ace held up the keys, then shut Scott's and Mr. White's eyes. "Don't worry Scott we're gonna ride for you! Come on let's roll."

"Where are we going, I thought that we were gonna get something to eat?" Sammy asked.

"Do you want to eat, or do you want to go check the drawers in the vault?" Big Ace said as he held up the keys.

"Yeah, you're a criminal for real! No wonder why your ass was in jail" Sammy said as he started laughing.

"Shut up before you get us caught, and watch my back."

"I got you, I'm shooting the first muthafucka I see, bad or good, I don't give a fuck right now. They won't kill my black ass and then throw me in a pile of dead bodies. I ain't going out like that."

"Shhh....I hear someone!" Big Ace whispered as he peeped around the corner and seen two Terrorist posted by the down stair entrance to the restaurant eating and drinking. "It's two of them by the restaurant entrance" Big Ace whispered.

"Man let's get them muthafucka, if they caught us slipping then they'd kill us," Sammy whispered.

"O'kay on three! One, two, three" Big Ace said as they turned the corner together and started unloading their AR-15 rifles with a silencers all up in the Terrorist body and face.

"Yeah, that's for Scott bitch!" Sammy yelled.

As three more Terrorist ran out of the restaurant bustin back.

"Shit!" Big Ace said as he snatched Sammy and pulled him around the wall just in time.

"Damn, good looking out! I owe you one," Sammy said.

"You owe me two," Big Ace said as he held his 45 automatic around the corner and let off the whole clip.

"Damn fool, you just alerted the whole damn Casino, use the got-damn silencer," Sammy yelled as they started running.

* * * *

"Did you guys hear that?" James asked.

"Yeah I heard it!" Eve said

"The police must've made it in!" Bill assumed.

"Yeah, that's our window of opportunity. Let's go get the hostages" James said eagerly.

"I'm with you!" Yvonne said.

"Me too!" said Eve.

"I don't care what we do, let's just do something." Bill said as they started creeping toward the backside of the second theatre thru the staff entrance.

"Follow my lead!" James whispered.

* * * *

Abby Shakur and everyone in the ballroom heard the loud shots being fired. Then a call came over the military radio. "We got two armed black men running toward the stairwell, Team Six needs back up."

Abby called two of his trusted comrades and said, "Catch them and kill them, and bring them back to me!"

"Yes Sir!" the two Terrorist said as they ran out.

Abby's right hand man got off the cell phone and walked over to Abby and whispered in his ear. "They stole all the money from all the bank accounts, trashed the system and took the detonators off the bombs."

"I want you to take four of our best men and hunt them down, and get my shit back. Torture them if you need to, but don't kill them until you get our stuff back!"

"O'kay!" The right hand man said as he pointed to four of the ten Terrorist who was in the ballroom and they all walked out.

The Governor said, "Looks like you're having a little problem," and laughed.

Abby turned toward him and said, "not as bad as yours" and shot the governor in the stomach with his big 40 gloc that had a silencer. Then laughed as the President rushed over to the Governor looked at his wound and started to apply pressure to it.

"That was foolish of you!" The President said!

* * * *

"Team Six where are you?" Abby's right hand man asked thru the radio.

"We're headed up the stairwell in pursuit of the two assailants"

"Do not kill them, just try to apprehend them, I repeat don't kill them. I'm on my way."

"Copy Team Leader."

* * * *

"Did you hear that?" Big Ace said out of breath.

"Yeah I heard it, we got to get them before they catch us" Sammy said.

"Come on this way!" Big Ace said as him and Sammy ran onto the sixth floor and down to the end of the hall and turned the corner onto the other hallway and posted up and waited.

"They're on the six floor," One of the mask Terrorist who was in pursuit of Big Ace and Sammy said over the radio.

"Copy, Team Leader said as he hurried up and got on the elevator and pushed the button to the six floor. The elevator slowed down and stopped on the sixth floor. "I'm in the elevator on the sixth floor now," the Team Leader said thru the radio.

"Copy, we're approaching the sixth floor now from the stairwell."

"Copy"

"Big Ace if I die then make sure that you give my cut to my baby's momma and kids for me," Sammy said.

"O'kay homie, I'll do that for you."

"If you die, who do you want me to give your cut too?" Sammy asked.

"If I die, then you keep my cut and ball out for me" Big Ace whispered.

"Damn. You make me want to kill you my damn self!"

"What!"

"I'm just kidding! You my man," Sammy said as he laughed.

"Be quiet!" Big Ace said as they heard the two Terrorists talking on the radio.

"Some are coming out of the elevator too!"

"Look!" Sammy said as he pointed to the service door.

"What?"

"The keys, the keys, you got the keys to the door."

Big Ace smiled as the elevator opened up, then pulled out the keys that he got off Mr. White's dead body.

"Go and open up the door, I'll hold them off!" Sammy said as Big Ace ran to the door and Sammy said "O'kay bitches, let's party" and shot rounds of bullets from his AR-15 rifle into the elevator just as two Terrorists was trying to step out and around into the cut. The round of bullets hit one Terrorist in motion, and knocked him back into the elevator as the other one dove on the ground and all of the Terrorists returned fire as Sammy jumped back behind the wall just in time.

"Come on!" Big Ace called out as he held the door open.

Sammy grabbed his fat 40 gloc with the silencer and reached around the wall and let off the whole clip back at the Terrorists, then turned and ran to the door as they returned fire.

They both laughed as they ran down the dark staircase, back down towards the bottom floor.

* * * *

"I want them drones in the air now." The General said as two of his Lieutenants put two helicopters drones in the sky equipped with infer-red thermal scope and a four round clip that shoot 30/30 bullets from a six inch barrel equipped with a fourteen inch silencer.

The drones disappeared in the sky as the General, FBI Agent, SWAT Lieutenant, Captain and two Secret Service Agents watched the picture of the camera that the drones was displaying on two thirty inch monitors, in the back of a big army equipment truck. The drones flew forty stories in the sky, and then started to descend down upon the roof top of the Casino. Drone number one, saw a man on the roof top of the Casino smoking a cigarette.

"There's one!" The FBI Agent said with excitement.

"There's another one" the Captain said.

"We see them!" The General said. "Now switch to thermal scope Lieutenant!" The Lieutenant hit two switches and two more figures were seen hiding in the cut. "O'kay, we see them all now! They're spread far apart, so hit two in the back that are on the roof top then, hit the ones up front.

"Yes Sir" both of the drones operators Lieutenants said, as they took off the thermal scope imaging and locked on the targets from seventy yards away.

"I'm locked on Sir!"

"I am too Sir!"

"Fire!" The General said as the Drones shot together and the 30/30 bullets whistled through the air and hit their targets in the chest and head. Blowing ones brains out and the other one had a hole in his back the size of a tennis ball killing them both instantly.

"Good hit, now take out the third and fourth target." The drones locked on to both of the Terrorists and the General gave the order, and the drones killed the other two Terrorist with one shot.

"Now scan the roof top one more time." The General ordered. "Good, now let's take a look around the Casino" The General order, just then there was a knock at the door.

"Who is it?" The General yelled.

"It's Major Nelson Sir," replied a guard who was stationed outside the door.

"Let the Major in!"

"Sir, we found a bomb in a gray Lincoln Navigator truck forty yards from here parked next to the Casino." The Major said.

"How big is it?" The General asked.

"From what I notice, it could take the whole side of the Casino out."

"Lieutenant, send the Drone down there and let's have a look at it, you stay scanning the Casino." The General ordered his other Drones operation Lieutenants. "O'kay, there's the gray Navigator. Hit the thermal scope scan! O'kay, it's hot! Send a bomb expert over and tell him, no need to suit up because if it goes off, we're all dead anyway. And send a twenty men crew around to each vehicle, look inside for explosives and tell them to be inconspicuous"

"Yes Sir!" The Major said as he ran out.

"Gentlemen, this is your opportunity to jump ship and get your men out. No telling how this night will end. Lieutenants, I want you men to scan each one of these vehicles with your thermal scanner, let's see if any more bombs are around here before we find out the wrong way." Everyone inside the truck looked around at each other spooked.

* * * *

James put his key into the door and slowly turned the lock as he twisted the knob on the door slowly at the same time. He knew if anyone was posted at the back door of the theatre, then he was considered dead. He peeped in and didn't see anything, so he slid in with his AR-15 rifle aimed in shooting form. His feet held the door open while Bill and Eve came in next, then Yvonne slid in as she kneeled down and squatted low ready to shoot. She closed the door quietly as they all scrambled to the far corner of the theatre. James crept along the edge of the wall and peeped around the corner. A restroom was at the back of the theatre where a few people were standing in line to use, and a Terrorist stood guard off to the side of the restroom with his back turned toward James. James saw Debbie standing in line escorting two old ladies, two people was in front, and one was in back of them. James made a small motion and Debbie caught it as she looked twice and vaguely smiled as she looked around nonchalantly and put her hands on her stomach holding up six fingers, then put her hands down so she wouldn't get caught. James shook his head and let her see the barrel of the gun. Two people came out of the restroom and they moved up next. James backed up to where Yvonne, Bill and Eve was waiting and said "It's only six of them. Eve I want you to stay back in the cut and watch our backs. If anyone comes thru the back door, then you shoot them o'kay?"

"O'kay"

"I want you to move on my command and shoot to kill!" James said.

"That's all I know!" Yvonne said as she gripped her AR-15 rifle.

"Let's do it!" Bill whispered.

James peeped back around the corner and Debbie was exiting the restroom trying not to look back. James waited until she was gone and two more men were waiting in line to use the restroom. James grabbed one of the show girls black dress off the floor and wrapped it around the barrel of his 40 gloc silencer and tipped toed around the corner as Yvonne was in back of him watching his back with her AR-15 rifle aimed high. James held his finger to his lips to notify the two men to be quiet, and one man started holding is chest breathing hard as the Terrorist stared at him trying to see if he was faking. Then suddenly he felt a vibe and he turned to look, and James shot him right in the forehead, and caught him before he could hit the floor, James laid the Terrorist body down slow.

"We're on your side," one of the men whispered as James grabbed the Terrorist Tec-9 and two extra clips and walked over to the men and asked how many are in there?

"Five more," one around the corner and two more by the front door."

"Thank you!"

"You need our help?" The Black Man who was playing like he had a breathing problem asked.

James said, "we got this, you stay out of the way."

"O'kay" the Black Man said as James, Yvonne and Bill started to creep down the big hallway of the theatre. Then they heard someone say "She having a heart attack, please someone help her!"

The Terrorist was trying to look as one ran over to see what was going on. James and Yvonne seen their opportunity and they ran out and both shot the two Terrorists that was standing in front of the theatre hitting them both multiple times as the Terrorists that was closest to them standing on the stage turned to shoot, and Bill unloaded his AR-15 rifle in the Terrorist body wildly. The Terrorist that ran over to see what was going on looked up then suddenly, when he went to aim his gun, a mob of terrified hostages that were being held began attacking him. A big White Man grabbed is gun and wrestled with it as a big Black Man socked the Terrorist twice in the face so hard, that you could hear his face crack. The Terrorist fell to the ground and a big White Man snatch the Tec-9 from him while a heavy set Black Man grabbed his 40 gloc from his waist, then several other hostages started to stomp him to death. Yvonne had her gun on the two men who snatch his guns. "It's o'kay Yvonne, they wouldn't be attacking him if they were on his side." Yvonne vaguely lowered her rifle as Janet and Debbie came running up hugging James and thanking Yvonne and Bill. James pointed at five men who were stomping the Terrorist out. "You four go get those guns off them two back there, and you take this one." And he gave the other Tec-9 that he got off the first Terrorist to a big Mexican looking gang banger.

"Listen, we got to get you guys out of here. It's not safe! There's Terrorist posted in the lobby that we got to kill to get out, so you guys with the guns got to help us.

You shoot to kill and watch each other's back. Time is of the essence, so we don't have none to waste. You four will come with us. We'll bring the fight to them. Bill..., You and Eve watch our backs, and once we make a way, then send these people out and all of you will have to run to the front entrance where the police are waiting. Help the old people and stay moving low and quick! Come on all of you we're going out the front door, stay quiet and Bill wait until we give you the signal before you send them out, and shoot anyone who shows up.

"Got you buddy" Bill said as he put another clip into his AR-15 rifle.

Yvonne smiled and shook her head.

Chapter 8

"Abby Sir, the United Kingdom Prime Minister and the Israel President's people both sent a billion dollars to the bank account that we requested" one of the Terrorist whispered into Abby's ear.

"Nobody's moving yet, and find out how much longer it's gonna take for them to get the computer system back up and running." Abby whispered back as the Terrorist walked to the back of the ballroom to call up stairs on his military radio, so none of the Leaders wouldn't hear the conversation.

"Team Nine, this is Team Leader One. How much longer is it gonna take you to finish that job?"

"Team Leader One, we are almost finish, but will only have one eye open at a time."

"Copy Team Nine!"

* * * *

"Oh shit," Bill cursed before they exited the theatre.

"What? Bill" James asked.

"That was Mr. Quick voice that just came over the radio. I think that he's trying to fix the computer so they

119

can use the cameras in the Casino and secure the doors." Bill said.

"Well, we better hurry then, come on let's do it!" James said as he glanced at Janet and Debbie and smiled, then slowly opened up the theatre double doors as he and Yvonne lead the way with four other armed hostages following them close behind. James held up his hand, and then put up two fingers. The Terrorists were spread out into two separate vantage points, at the front entrance and alongside the walls, but they were still visible, because James and Yvonne was entering from the rear lobby.

Yvonne looked around the corner and saw four Terrorist reflections off of a slot machine standing together talking. She held up four fingers, then laid on the ground and crawled over by a table that was fifteen feet away. James covered her with his AR-15 rifle pointed at the one who was sitting down on the table, as he smoked a cigarette. Yvonne crawled to another vantage point and signaled for James, James whispered to the big Black and White Man who attacked the Terrorist in the theatre and said, "You go crawl over to that area where those slot machines are and try to be quiet." They shook their heads and went down on the floor and started crawling. The White Man made it, but the Terrorist saw a glimpse of something, it was the big Black Man's ass that came up too high, and the Terrorist stood up to look and James shot him right in the head knocking his brains all over the slot machines that was in back of him. The noise from the silencer alerted the other four Terrorist who looked over toward the sound of the noise, clinching their guns but they were too slow and the first two got hit. Yvonne shot three quick shots hitting her first target in the face blowing the back of his head out and her other two shots hit the second Terrorist in the chest area dropping him dead as the other two Terrorist dove out of the way and rolled by the slot machines. James ran toward the other side of the Casino and shot at the one Terrorist who was at the other end. The Terrorist ducked down as one of James bullets hit him in the shoulder, and knocked him to the ground.

Another Terrorist was sitting behind one of slot machines eating as the shooting started, and he jumped up and saw James in motion and shot at him as bullets whistled by James head. The big white boy had seen the Terrorist jump up and start shooting at James, and unloaded his clip all into the Terrorist body. Two more Terrorists ran out from the restaurant and the big Black Man caught them in motion as he sat up from the ground and unloaded his 40 gloc on them, the Mexican and the other Black Man who was with them helped gun down the other two Terrorist as well.

One of the Terrorist jumped up from in back of the slot machine and tried to shot, but Yvonne was waiting and shot him right between the eyes as soon as he popped his head up. The other Terrorist jumped on the military radio and started yelling, "we're under attack, there in the..." (Pow, Pow, Pow) James ran over and dove into the aisle and shot the Terrorist three times with his 40 gloc before he landed on the ground. "CLEAR!" James said as he spun around in a circle looking for any other Terrorist. Yvonne was scoping out the surroundings as well.

Then she said, "I'm clear too!"

"Tell Bill to come on" James yelled. As all hostages started running out and thru the entrance way. The young were carrying the old, and everybody was moving fast. It was close to 150 people and it looked like a stampede as they moved thru the Casino lobby.

James was the closes to the door as Yvonne was in the middle behind a slot machine, and Bill and the other armed men were scattered out in different areas with their firearms reloaded cocked and ready to shoot.

Janet and Debbie stopped by James and Janet said, "Are you coming with us?" Knowing in her heart that she already knew the answer.

"No, I got some unfinished business to handle, ya'll go help take care of these people. I'll catch up to you soon." James said as he looked her in the eyes and she hugged and kissed him, and said, "Hurry up o'kay!"

"I will!" James smiled

Debbie kissed James on the lips and said, "I'll be waiting for you!"

James smiled as they ran off. The last of the hostages was running out as the five armed men looked at James and James pointed for them to leave too, as they all ran out. Bill and Eve ran up to James as Yvonne walked over to them with her gun focused on the entrances of the hallways. Eve said, "We're staying with you!"

"No you guys go help the police figure out what's going on, we got this" James said.

"Are you sure?" Bill asked.

"Yeah I'm sure, now go!" James yelled as Eve kissed him and he said, "Now hurry up!"

"Give me a kiss Yvonne!" Bill asked as he puckered his lips out.

"Get out of here boy!" Yvonne said as she laughed Bill and Eve ran out just as the security gate started to close. But, they beat the gate just in time. "We got company" Yvonne said as she picked off one of the two men that was running up on them down the hallway.

The other man jumped inside a doorway when he saw his partner get shot, and he started to shoot back as James and Yvonne ran toward the back way and ducked behind some slot machined. James saw the dead man on the ground and grabbed his three extra clips. When a voice came over the military radio and said, "Team Four, they are behind the back slot machines."

James looked at Yvonne and said, "the cameras are on now, let's go" and they both ran thru the back of the Casino and ducked off into the back stairwell.

"I lost them Team Four, keep your eyes open." A voice replied over the military radio.

"You are my damn eyes fool! Where are they?" The Terrorist said as he glanced down at his partner and seen the big hole in his forehead.

"I only got one computer so be patient." The voice said.

"Did you hear that? They only have one computer monitor to look at, so they have to look all over for us." Yvonne said.

"That should make it a lot easier for us, but we need to get to that computer room and destroy it again."

"That might be our best move. It can't be too many more of them around here now," Yvonne said.

"I think you might be right let's go see!" James said as he smiled at her.

* * * *

Big Ace and Sammy was headed to the vault where all the gamblers and hotel high rollers kept all their expensive jewelry. They walked up to the vault entrance and heard some people already in the vault. Big Ace held up his finger to his lips and peeped in. It was three Terrorist in the vault opening the medal boxes and taking the valuables out. "It's three!" Big Ace counted as him and Sammy walked in with their guns drawn.

"Drop my muthafucken shit bitch!" Sammy said as the Terrorist with the bag of jewelry threw the bag at them and rushed them. The bag hit Big Ace in the face and Sammy saw the bag and ducked. The Terrorist grabbed the barrel of Sammy's Tech-9 silencer as Sammy and Big Ace both let off two bullets. Sammy's bullet hit one of the Terrorist in the chest killing him on the spot and Big Ace bullets ricocheted off the steal vault boxes as the other Terrorist grabbed Big Ace's, AR-15 rifle and tried to twist it out of his hands. Big Ace kneed him in the balls and head butted him as he fell out cold. The other Terrorist was socking Sammy in the face as Big Ace shot him in the head and said "Get off my homeboy fool!" Then looked at the other one who was dazed laying on the floor, "you alright little homie!"

"Yeah, I'm cool!"

"Grab this fool's hand gun" Big Ace told Sammy.

As Sammy walked over to the Terrorist and grabbed his big Desert Eagle off his side and started pistol whooping him. "You fucked my job up, killed my little white homeboy, and killed that thick bad bitch that I wanted to fuck." Sammy said as he beat him with the gun.

"Let me get some! You tried to steal our jewelry, and killed all them innocent people, you crazy muthafucka." Big Ace said as he was stomping and kicking the Terrorist in the face.

"If you kick him one more time I'll blow your brains out." A voice said as Big Ace froze with his foot in the air over the man's face. "Put your hands in the air, and don't move."

"O'kay man, don't shoot! You guys can have the damn jewels, me and my friend will just leave you here to do what you're here to do." Big Ace reasoned.

The Terrorist removed Big Ace and Sammy guns, and the Leader said, "Am afraid it's not that easy. See you guys got something of ours and we want it back." The Terrorist picked up their partner off the floor and his face was busted, swollen and fucked up. He pushed off the two Terrorist that picked him up and spit out two teeth as he glared over at Big Ace and Sammy.

"Damn, my bad! I trip out like that sometimes." Big Ace said, but just as the words was coming out of Big Ace's mouth the Terrorist socked Big Ace in the jaw knocking him to the ground.

The Terrorist was about to continue when the Leader said, "WAIT" and the Terrorist looked over at him and was breathing hard. "Now, give us the codes and the detonator, or my friend here will spend all night torturing you!"

"What codes and detonators?" Big Ace said.

Sammy mouthed off and said, "That's right homie don't give them shit," then looked at Big Ace, as the

Leader slapped Sammy with the barrel of his 45 automatic that had the silencer extension on it.

"Damn that hurt," Sammy screamed. "I knew I should've stuck to drug dealing."

"I advise you to hand over the codes and detonators now!"

Big Ace looked at him and said, "Fuck you, we're not giving you shit!"

"We'll see about that! They're all yours." The Leader said as the Terrorist who was getting stomped out by Big Ace smiled, with his face swollen and his two front teeth gone. He went at Big Ace as another big muscular Terrorist walked towards Sammy and they both started whooping on Big Ace and Sammy ass.

"Do you want to talk now?" The Leader said as he held his hand up.

"Fuck you bitch, we ain't giving you shit!" Sammy said as he spit blood out of his mouth. "Proceed then!" The Leader said as the Terrorist started whooping Big Ace and Sammy ass some more.

"Put your fucken guns down or I'll blow your heart out your chest." James said as him and Yvonne was standing in back of the Terrorists as they were caught slipping with their backs turned watching their comrades whoop the two black men ass. The Leader brung four men with him, plus the one that Big Ace and Sammy was whooping made five. Three of the Terrorist tried to spin around and shoot, but Yvonne and James dropped them before they even completed the turn.

"Does anyone else want to try it?" James said as he looked at Big Ace and Sammy and said "get their guns.

"That's right," Big Ace said as he snatched the Leaders gun. Sammy grabbed the gun off the man who was whooping his ass and started pistol whooping him as he fell to the ground.

"Man I'm glad ya'll came! These muthafucka was about to kill us" Big Ace said as he slapped the Leader across the nose with the hand gun breaking his shit. Then he looked at the one who was whooping his ass and shot him in the face three times.

Sammy was kicking the other one in the corner, then stopped to catch his breath and said "I'm getting to old for this shit", and shot the man five times and said "Bitch ass muthafucka."

"What are you gonna do with him?" Big Ace asked.

"I know what I'm gonna do with him." Sammy said as he started walking toward the Leader.

"Wait!" James said as he pulled off the Leader's ski mask. "Mr. Faller, how did I know that that was you? It looks like your plan has taken a turn for the worse."

"I knew we shouldn't have hired you! I had a gut feeling that you were trouble. But Kerr had the hot's for that stupid sister of yours, and fucked up our whole plan." Mr. Faller said as he stared up at James.

"But Mr. Cin didn't like you either, he knew that you were up to no good." James was fishing now for more information.

"Cin was a fool! He was totally blinded. He even brung the detonators in without even knowing what he had. He was just a young fool leaching off his family's wealth. A fucking parasite! He's lucky that I just left him handcuffed in his office. I should've killed him too."

"Well, I'm sorry to inform you that, your killing days are over with. He's all yours!" James said as he stepped back and Big Ace and Sammy smiled through their badly swollen faces. And begin to whoop on Mr. Faller.

Mr. Faller said "But you're a police you got to arrest me."

"I'm not anymore! I got fired remember." James said as him and Yvonne laughed.

"Ouch, ouch, stop it, please." Mr. Faller said as Big Ace and Sammy was stomping his body.

"Let me get some!" Sammy said as he started slapping Mr. Faller in the face with the big Desert Eagle. "I'm tired!" Sammy said as Big Ace smiled and aimed his gun at Mr. Faller's head and when he looked up, Big Ace pulled the trigger.

"Are you gonna be alright?" James asked Big Ace and Sammy.

"Yeah we got this now! Thank you for having our backs, we were almost dead." Big Ace said as he shook James hand.

"Yeah we owe you one!" Sammy said.

Listen, we got to go try to finish this shit. You be careful because they got the cameras up and running. But it's only one screen, so they got to flip through three hundred cameras to find you. They're on the twelfth floor working the computer.

"Gotch you! Ya'll be careful too!" Sammy said as James and Yvonne departed.

"They're up to something!" Yvonne said as they walked away.

"Yeah, why else would they be in a vault?" James joked as they smiled and turned the corner.

* * * *

"Come on grab that bag of jewels and follow me! And stay on point this time, you almost got us killed back there." Big Ace said as he scolded Sammy.

"Yeah, cause he beat the shutout of you, he was whoopin you ass!" Sammy joked as he laughed.

"You need to look in the mirror, because it looks like Mike Tyson gotta' hold of your ass!" Big Ace joked back and laughed.

"Is it bad?"

"Hell yeah! You got a pumpkin face for real." (Ha, Ha) Big Ace and Sammy cracked-up as they crept into the customer's restroom.

"Why are we in here?" Sammy asked.

"Because it's no cameras, now let's see what's in the bag!"

"Damn, look at my face!" Sammy said when he looked in the mirror.

"I told you!"

"You're fucked up too!" Sammy said.

"I knew it because, my whole face is numb! It feels like I got on a Halloween mask." Big Ace said as he poured out the jewels on the counter. All kinds of big diamond rings, necklaces, bracelets and earrings, and two suede black bags. Big Ace poured out the contents in one of the suede bags and it was ten 5 carat princess cut diamonds.

"Damn, now that's money there!" Sammy said.

Then he poured out the other suede bag and it was ten 5 carat yellow canary cut diamonds in it.

"We rich!" Sammy shouted.

"Not yet, but we will be!" Big Ace grabbed the condom machine and busted it open. Then start putting the princess cut diamonds in one as he tied it in a knot, then took another condom and wrapped it up again and tide another knot.

"That's too big to swallow Homie," Sammy said.

"I know that's why it's going up the back way."

"You're putting it up your ass?" Sammy asked.

"You got a better idea?" Listen when the police come in here they most likely gonna search us. And the three Rolex watches that you're wearing is not gonna look good. But I know they're not gonna find these and it's on..! I'm gonna be the ghost inside, the Rolls Royce Ghost!" Big Ace said as he busted-up laughing.

"Here do these too, because I'm not leaving this muthafucka empty handed. We're gonna ball together." Sammy said.

"Smart guy," Big Ace said as he put two condoms over the other yellow diamonds and gave them to Sammy.

"This is kind of big!" Sammy squirmed.

"More money!" Big Ace said as he put on some diamond pieces and put the ones in his pocket in the leather bag. Sammy did the same. As Big Ace found a place in the ceiling and put the rest of the jewels, then went into the stall and pushed the condom full of diamonds up in his rectum. He came out and Sammy went to do the same thing and then walked out smiling as he tried to give Big Ace some dap. "Fool, wash your hands so we can go handle this business and get the hell out of here. I got big plans now!"

"Me too playa," Sammy said as he dried his hands off and gave Big Ace dap.

"Let's go!" Big Ace said as they peeped out the restroom door, and then crept out.

Chapter 9

The police had all of the hostages rounded up and safe as they started questioning them. Bill and Eve was providing the General, Captain, FBI and Secret Service with as much information as they could.

"Now let me get this straight!" The FBI Agent said. You two with Mr. Pryor who is the Casino security, and Ms. Yvonne Bay who is the Secret Service Agent, was the one's who was shooting it out with the Terrorists, you interrupted the Terrorists scheme to electronically steal money from the banks all over the world, which you guys believe was the Terrorists main objective, and you did it by downloading all of the money that they already stolen into Ms. Yvonne Bay bank account, in Washington D.C. Bank Of America Trust, then you guys found 3 big barrels of explosives that Ms. Yvonne Bay disarmed and took the detonators switches off, then you hide the switches in a safe place in the first theatre, then went and shot it out with the Terrorists that was holding the hostages, and after saving the hostages you had another shoot out with some more Terrorists in the lobby and after killing them off, you escorted the hostages out the front entrance here where the law enforcement officers detained you."

"Right!" Bill said as Eve shook her head.

"And you and Ms. Yvonne Bay are the ones who disabled the computer system."

"Correct," Bill said.

"So how many Terrorists do you think that you've killed during all of these shoot-outs?" The General asked.

Bill thought about the question then said, "Ms. Yvonne Bay and James Pryor were really doing all the killings, they're like sharp shooters. I might have shot two or three Terrorists in self-defense of course, but they killed around 20 or better easy. But it was two other Black men in their warring with the Terrorists as well. We kept hearing the Terrorists talk about them over the radio, and they must've been train too, because they were causing havoc too!" Bill explained as Eve shook her head in agreement.

An officer ran up and gave the Secret Service Agent a sheet of paper, and the Secret Service Agent said. "Wow" As he showed his partner and then handed the sheet of paper to the General.

"Well, I see that you did a real good job with your computer skills, because Ms. Yvonne Bay seems to be the wealthiest woman in the world." The General handed the FBI Agent the paper and said, "Make sure that you put a freeze on that account."

"Yes Sir" the FBI Agent said when he saw all the billions of dollars in her account.

"So you believe that the ransom for the hostage was just a camouflage, to buy them some time while they steal all this money, then blow up the Casino and the Leaders and hostages as they make their escape?"

"Yes that was James assumption. He said that it was also a very well planned out scheme considering that half the Terrorists worked at the Casino as part of the Elite Security Team. James said that the heads of security Mr. Faller and Mr. Quick had to be in on it, for the Terrorists to get the bombs in and know how to operate the electronic banking systems like that." Bill explained.

"That's sounds like a logical assumption from my perception as well" The General stated. "So tell me why did, Mr. Pryor and Ms. Bay decide to stay in the Casino instead of leaving with you and the others?"

"Well they said that they had to save the United States President and the other Leaders." Bill said.

"That sounds like everything we need to know, if we have any more questions, then we'll call you back. There's some food and some drinks for everyone at the vendors trucks, please help yourself." The FBI Agent said.

"O'kay thank you!" They said as they left out.

"What do you think General?" The FBI Agent asked.

"I think Mr. Pryor and Ms. Bay is our blessing in disguise, because they can't hold us accountable for the people that are already trapped in the Casino. They got a right to fight for their lives, they just didn't expect for two military special trained officers to be running loose. The General and the officers laughed. "Listen Captain Fields, get me four of your best SWAT Team Members ready, because as soon as we get the signal from that military radio we're going in.

"They'll be on point and ready for your command General." The Captain said as he walked out.

* * * *

James and Yvonne was walking by the restaurant on their way to the ballroom, when James saw a movement on the side refrigerator soft drink stand. James held up his hand, and then crept into the restaurant when he saw an older Black Man had his back turned grabbing juices and bottles of water out of the soft drink stand. "If you move, I'll kill you!" James said as Yvonne held her gun up in her shooting stand looking for anyone who might be with the man.

"Please don't shoot me." The man begged as he looked up.

"Who are the drinks for?" James asked.

The man looked at James then Yvonne, and then knew that they didn't look like the Terrorists but couldn't take any chances. "They're for me!"

"That's a lot of drinks for just one person. But im'ma tell you what I think you're doing, and that's running errands for the Terrorists," James said.

"Oh no, I wouldn't do that! I'm just trying to get something to drink and eat for me and my friends. We don't want any trouble from no-one." The man explained in a scared voice.

"Lift up your shirt slowly!" O'kay, now show us were you and your friends are hiding."

"We don't want no problem Sir, we just came to gamble!"

"We're not gonna hurt you, we're the good guys." James said with a smile on his face.

Yvonne spotted a Terrorist walking by the slot machine and said "Get down!" and James squatted down watching the Terrorist creep by as Yvonne took aim and shot him right in the side of the head. Then she moved quickly by the wall to make sure that no one else wasn't with him. "He was alone!" Yvonne whispered as she kept her gun trained on the outside machines.

"Now do you believe us?" James asked the man.

"Yeah, I sure believe you now."

"Well grab your stuff and lead the way."

"What floor are you guys on."

"The second floor"

"How many of you guys are there?

"Nine counting me!"

"Is it clear Yvonne?" James asked.

"Yeah we clear!"

"O'kay, come on - what's your name?"

"Ron."

"O'kay let's get the hell out of here Ron." Ron led the way with drinks and left over food in his pillow case. They went thru the stairwell on the second floor and Ron knocked four times then twice and an older black lady opened-up the door and was startled when she saw James and Yvonne with him.

"It's o'kay baby, they're the good guys." And they rushed in and closed the door behind themselves.

James looked around and seen two more old couples and three young girls in their twenties, one of the girls was Robin, the girl that he met in the staff lounge when Big Ace walked over to the table trippin'.

"Oh James, it's good to see you! It's alright; he's security in the Casino. I know him he's a good guy." Robin said to the old people as Ron started handing out to everyone a juice or water.

"Hi Robin, I'm glad to see that you guys are safe, is anybody else on this floor?" James asked.

"Not that we know of." Robin said.

James looked out of the window and seen that they were only two stories away from the outside landing and said, "I got an idea. Yvonne cover me!" He peeped out the door and saw that it was clear before he exited, and jogged down to the maids linen closet and grabbed twenty new sheets, then jogged back and went inside of the room while Yvonne stood in the doorway listening for any intruders.

"What is she doing, and why does she have the door open?" An old lady cried out.

"She's watching our backs to make sure no Terrorist can creep up on us," James said with a smile.

"Oh that's smart, can she shoot that big gun?" The old lady asked.

141

"She's one of the best!" James said as Yvonne turned and smiled at him. James started tying the sheets together in knots, and then putting a military loop knotted at the end. Then had the old men pull the sheets in a tug-of-war to make sure that the knots were strong enough. Now who's first?"

"What are you gonna do?" The old lady asked.

"He's gonna lower us down to safety Helen, we're going home baby, so don't be scared."

"I don't want to go first." Helen boldly stated.

"I'll go first since I'm the heaviest," the big bald head White Man said. "Just let the ladies go next, and I'll help you from the bottom."

"O'kay James said as they put him in the bottom loop of the sheets and lowered him down to the ground with two other men.

"See Helen, it's easy and if it could hold big Ed, then you know that it will hold anyone of you ladies. Now come on," Helen put the loop around her as she held on for dear life, and they lowered her quickly, then the next old lady. Three police ran over to assist them as James lowered the last two men. The police called for James to climb down and James said, "I got to go save the President, I'll shut-off the security systems so you guys can get in o'kay!"

The officers gave James a thumbs-up as a drone flew up and hovered in one spot and James returned the thumbs-up, and walked away as him and Yvonne crept down the hallway toward the stairwell.

* * * *

"Did you guys see that, that was one of our Secret Service Agent with him by the door that was Yvonne Bay." The Secret Service Agent said with a proud smile.

"Yeah, they're truly very courageous soldiers. Lieutenant send that data to the Pentagon NOW," the General said.

"Go interview the people who were just saved, and see if they have any information." The FBI Agent said as a police ran in out of breath and started talking.

"Sir, Officer Pryor said that he would disable the security system so we can gain access without detection."

"Good, get the Teams in place, it's time to put an end to this nonsense once and for all," the General said as he jumped up and walked out of the back of a military truck.

Chapter 10

"Look!" Sammy said.

"What?" Big Ace said as he lifted his rifle up ready to shoot.

"Over there! Watch my back." Sammy said as he jogged over by the dead Terrorist that was laying in the lobby by the slot machine. Sammy bent down and picked up a short tube.

Big Ace walked over with his rifle up ready to shoot and said, "What is that?"

"It's a rocket launcher it's called " ALAW" which stands for " Light Anti Tank Weapon" Sammy said as he smiled and put the strap around his shoulder, so it could hang off his back.

"What are you gonna do with that?"

"Well my good friend, the computer room is bullet proof, but not rocket proof, so what do you say we go and blow their asses up?" Sammy said as he smiled.

"Now that's gangsta! Let's go!" Big Ace said as they headed to the elevator.

* * * *

James and Yvonne were creeping up the stairwell headed to the twelfth floor to take out the computer. They made it up to the twelfth floor with no problems. James cracked the stairwell door that was angled sideways from the computer room, so James had to peep out down the hall around fifty yards away, and saw six Terrorist standing guard outside of the locked door. Mr. Quick office was across from the computer room, and a Terrorist was sitting in Mr. Quick office doorway. Mr. Quick was seen moving around in the computer room. The elevator was ten feet away from the stairwell door, and the wall across from the stairwell had an indentation in the wall where a big plant was sitting in a big clay pot for decoration.

"I'm going across the hall to that dented space; you shoot from here and watch your back!" James whispered.

"O'kay!" Yvonne said as James smiled at her and walked out shooting his rifle as he strolled across the hallway. Yvonne was on point as she leaned out the stairwell door and started picking off the Terrorists that was in her sight. James picked off the first two Terrorists as he walked out spraying wildly. The Terrorist who was in the doorway dove back into the office as James started shooting. Two Terrorists jumped up with their rifles in hand as Yvonne picked them both off. The one that was in the office leaned out of the doorway and started shooting his Tec-9 as Yvonne and James jumped back. The other Terrorist jumped up from the ground and ran into the little dented space where the water fountain was located, and started shooting toward the wall space where James was located.

"Damn, Damn! This really wasn't a good idea!" James said as bullets ate up the wall where he was hiding at. He reloaded his AR-15 rifle when he heard a voice come over the military radio.

"Team Nine is taking heavy gun fire, need assistance! Over" Mr. Quick was looking out of the bullet proof window as the shootout was taking place. "Team One, we are taking heavy gun fire, need assistance!" Mr. Quick repeated over the radio.

"Did you hear that?" James asked Yvonne as she shook her head yes. James unloaded another clip into the bullet proof window, as Mr. Quick laughed and flipped James his middle finger.

"Shit we can't get to him!" James yelled to Yvonne as bullets ricocheted off the wall knocking patches of plaster all over the floor.

The elevator started coming up as the numbers started counting up and stopped at the twelfth floor. "Here they come" James said as Yvonne saw the elevator climb up too, and pointed her rifle at the elevator as James turned his back so that he was against the inner wall in the corner of the crevice, as the elevator door opened up.

A bloody Terrorist was standing up with his head bent down and Big Ace was behind him holding him up from behind with his AR-15 rifle held up under the dead Terrorist arms, then Big Ace started shooting wildly when the doors opened.

Yvonne saw the elevator doors open and a rifle firing from underneath a Terrorist arms, so she began shooting back at the dead Terrorist when his head exploded and Big Ace dropped him and the gun and fell back into the corner screaming, "it's us bitch, don't shoot" with the Terrorist blood splattered all over his face.

"Hold your fire Yvonne," James yelled as the Terrorists started shooting in the elevator.

James timed it and reached for his 45 automatic to pull it out and caught the Terrorist that was by the water fountain slippin and shot him four times in his bullet proof vest, knocking him to the ground. Yvonne leaned out and shot the Terrorist in his head with her Tec-9 rifle blowing his brains all over the carpet. The other Terrorist was reloading as Sammy held his rocket launcher out of the elevator and Big Ace said, "Wait!" as he dove out into the hallway and Yvonne started shooting at the Terrorist who was in the office reloading to keep him back. Mr. Quick eyes got big when he saw Sammy pointing the rocket launcher at the window, then he dove to the side just as Sammy pulled the trigger and fire shot out from behind the rocket launcher, and the rocket fired blowing the bullet proof glass and glass splattered everywhere, striking the Terrorist who was standing in the doorway in the face knocking him down. As James and Yvonne ran full speed toward the computer room, then James turned and shot the Terrorist who was laying on the floor, four time with his AR-15 rifle, and rush behind Yvonne as she was passing him up and ran into the computer room. Mr. Quick was on his back slightly dazed when Yvonne ran up on him and stood over him with her Tec-9 aimed at his face. James ran and looked in the restroom and seen a bunch of dead bodies piled up on the floor.

Big Ace and Sammy ran up excited. "Did you guys see that shit? That rocket blew the doors off this bitch." Sammy said full of excitement.

"Wait, wait don't shoot him yet!" Big Ace said as he leaned down and socked Mr. Quick three times in the face knocking him unconscious.

"Let me get some too," Sammy said as he started stomping Mr. Quick in the face.

"Hold up ya'll, hold up a minute!" James said as Mr. Quick was shaking off the daze. Yvonne walked back over to the entrance to the computer room and posted up watching their backs.

Big Ace seen Yvonne move and looked at Sammy and said, "now that's a down bitch!"

"You ain't lying! My type of woman." Sammy said.

James smiled at them as Mr. Quick looked up. "Mr. Quick! Tell me why I shouldn't torture you and kill you?"

"Come on James, I didn't want to hurt nobody." Mr. Quick said as he spit out some blood.

"Where is the rest of the bombs at?"

"Bombs! What bombs?" Big Ace said as he looked at James then Mr. Quick.

"You guys found them all!"

"I think you're lying, Fellas!" James said as he looked at Big Ace and Sammy.

Big Ace socked him twice in the eye and Sammy kicked him in the nuts as Mr. Quick screamed out in pain and curled up.

"Hold up, hold up ya'll! Now where are the other bombs at?" James asked again.

"I swear to you, there isn't anymore! You found them all in the basement. Mr. Faller brung them in two days ago." Mr. Quick said.

"Why did you hire a Terrorist group to take over the Casino? And who all was involved?" James asked.

Mr. Quick started laughing. "You really don't know what's going on huh? Your President and Leaders will all die tonight. Abby Shakur was a prisoner in Guantanamo Bay, and he's plotting to take his revenge on the United States and their allies. This Casino was his perfect plan, to steal billions of dollars from the banks around the world, and fund Terrorists group so they can have money and power to fight and defeat their enemies. It would have worked if Mr. Kerr didn't go tender dick, for that pretentious stuck-up sister of yours. Nonetheless, Abby Shakur will kill the Leaders and die a hero for his cause" and MR. Quick spit out some more blood as he laughed.

"Fellas he's all yours!" James said as he looked at Big Ace and Sammy.

"Oh you want to kill innocent people huh... I didn't like your punk ass anyway," Big Ace said as he started kicking Mr. Quick in the ribs and stomped his leg and broke it. Mr. Quick screamed out loud.

"Oh you want to holla like a bitch now. This is for little Scott and all of those innocent people you killed." Sammy said as he pistol whipped him in the head with the big Desert Eagle that he had. "Take that, and this! Put your hands down bitch."

Big Ace socked Mr. Quick in the nuts and he curled up and grabbed them as Sammy busted his head twice putting big gashes in his head as he slapped him with the gun.

"Wait a minute" Big Ace said. "I got a better idea! Drag his punk ass, we're taking him to the mile high club"

Sammy and Big Ace smiled as they drug his half unconscious body to his office window and they picked him up and threw him out of the twelfth story window. And a drone flew up as Sammy pulled out his Desert Eagle and Yvonne hollered "No, that's a military drone."

"Oh, I thought that the Aliens was coming to help them, I was about to knock that muthafucka out the sky!" And they laughed as they threw up their thumbs and gave the thumbs up sign. Then walked back to the computer room where James was flipping through the cameras and found the ballroom footage.

"Come and look Yvonne." James called as she walked over and Sammy went to go post up and watch their backs. "It looks like it's only seven Terrorist and their all spread out standing around the walls. The President and all of the Leaders are still alive, and that must be Abby Shakur sitting in the chair on the stage." James observed.

"We got to act fast" Yvonne said.

A voice came over the radio and said "Team Nine report! Team Nine report over."

James looked at the screen and saw a Terrorist at the back of the stage talking into the military radio and said "I got a plan." And picked up the military radio and said, "Mr. Quick had to fly out, so I don't think that he can speak." and Big Ace, Sammy and Yvonne all started laughing trying to cover up their sounds.

"Who is this!" the voice asked.

"Don't worry about who I am, let me speak to your boss!" James said.

The man walked over to Abby Shakur and he whispered into his ear then handed him the military radio. "I am the man in charge, who am I speaking too."

"Mr. Abby Shakur I presume!" James said.

"Yes, I see that you've been doing your homework, but who am I speaking too?"

"This is James Pryor Casino security!"

"So you are the one who's been running around killing my men?"

"Yes, that would be me! And frankly, I'm piss that you would come here and fuck up my new job like this. Now I don't know how I'm gonna pay my bills." James said as Big Ace and Sammy started busting up and Yvonne shook her head.

"Well James, I think that you have something that belongs to me, and I have something here you might want."

"Oh you must be talking about the detonators and the account information with the hundred and forty billion dollars in it." James asked.

"Yes, that would be accurate!"

"But what do you got for me?"

"Well how about the President of the United States?" Abby said.

"I didn't even vote for him, I voted for the other guy, and a hundred and forty billion dollars is a lot of money for him."

"Well who would you like to trade for, I got a variety of Leaders here who you might be interested in."

"Maybe we can trade. Do you by any chance got Mr. Kerr the owner of the Casino? He's a good man, I like him and my sister would be mad if I let him die like that. She really got feelings for the old guy. You know what I'm saying." James said as Yvonne swung her hand at him, and James made a face at her.

Abby looked at the radio then at Mr. Kerr, and Mr. Kerr smiled as he sat next to the United Kingdom Prime Minister and all the Leaders looked at Mr. Kerr, because everyone could hear the conversation taking place. "Yes, I got Mr. Kerr in here as well.

"Well, I tell you what! I got two bank account codes, one has a hundred billion in it, and the other one has the forty billions in it. I'll give you the forty billion for Mr. Kerr and I'll tell you where the detonators are at, so you can blow this bitch off the map...but after I leave! That way nobody would know about the hundred billions that I took, and I can live my life wealthy and having fun, while the Law Enforcement Agencies are chasing you. See the way I see it is, while the Law Enforcement Agencies are running around trying to figure out who all got killed in the big explosion. I'll be long gone and nothing can come back on me. You feel me?" James reasoned.

"So why do you want Mr. Kerr when he could be the one who could hurt you.

"Well he won't know that I kept the hundred billion dollars and he'll be so grateful that I saved him, he'll give me some money as a gift and no one will expect otherwise. See that's why your ass almost loss, because your ass don't think ahead. Mr. Kerr ain't listening is he?" James asked.

"No, no I'm in the back room!"

"O'kay cool, so we have a deal or what?"

"Sure it sounds good to me, why don't you come and bring me the stuff and you and Mr. Kerr can leave after." Abby said as he looked at the Leaders and they all were staring being caught up in the crazy conversation.

"Do you think that I'm stupid or something, like I'm gonna just walk in there and let you capture me and take everything? No you won't trick me like that!"

"So how do you suggest we do the exchange?" Abby asked.

"It got to be in an open area, like the bottom floor lounge area, that way I can see you and all of your flunkies and don't try nothing slick either, and let me speak to Mr. Kerr so I can make sure he's alive.

"Who is this?" James asked as he was watching them on camera.

"This is Mr. Kerr."

Mr. Kerr, this is James Pryor! Tell me what is my sister first name?"

"Hi James, its Janet! Mr. Kerr said.

"Mr. Kerr, how are you doing buddy? They didn't hurt you or nothing did they?" James asked.

"No James, I'm fine."

"Good, I'm coming to get you o'kay."

"O'kay!" Mr. Kerr said.

"You just hang in there buddy."

"O'kay"

"Now put Abby back on the radio."

"O'kay, here!" Mr. Kerr said as he gave the radio back to Abby.

"He's fine no problems." Abby said.

"O'kay, meet me in the bottom lounge in ten minutes and don't make me wait to long." James said.

"O'kay Mr. Pryor, but if you're playing games, then I'll kill everything that you love.... I promise you this."

"Just be there in ten minutes!" James said.

Abby Shakur got up and called three of his six comrades and pointed to the other ones and said something as the other three spread out in a triangle with their guns held ready to shoot. Abby grabbed Mr. Kerr and he followed his three armed comrades out of the double doors.

James looked at Yvonne and said "open up the front entrance." And she ran to the computer controls and pushed a lever back, as the security gate re-opened.

"Why didn't you just ask for the President?" Yvonne asked.

"Because he would've been a target if we tried to rescue him from Abby like that. Abby probably would've just killed him."

"Then why are we gonna save Mr. Kerr when we believe that he's involved." Big Ace said.

"We're not, we're gonna go save the President and all of the other Leaders, while the police can come in and deal with Abby and his crew." James flicked through the camera and saw Abby, Mr. Kerr, and the other three armed men walk out of the stairwell on the bottom floor and started walking toward the lobby.

They heard Sammy moving in back of them and when they looked, he was putting on a bullet proof vest that he took off one of the Terrorist.

"What are you doing?" Big Ace asked.

"What do it look like I'm doing, I'm not trying die. I got too much to look forward to. Them bullets ain't got no names on them!" Sammy said.

"Your absolutely right playa! Let me grab one too. Ya'll can act like you're bullet proof if you want to." Big Ace said as he went out and took a bullet proof vest off one of the other dead Terrorist.

"They might be right, we better grab one too." James said as Yvonne shook her head in agreement.

They all put on a bloody bullet proof vest, and James looked around and said "let's finish this!" And they all looked at each other and smiled as they crept down the hallway.

* * * *

"General, why do you think that he didn't want to trade the President for the money or the detonators?" The FBI Agent asked.

"Because he either didn't want to get the President caught up in a shootout, or he's going for the President." The General said.

"If he's with Yvonne, then 9 times out of 10 he's headed for the President!" The Secret Service Agent said.

A police in tactical gear ran inside of the Army Van and said. "The front entrance security gates just opened."

"He's sending Abby Shakur right into our hands, send both Assault Teams in now! He must be headed for the President and the other Leaders." The General stated as he smiled to himself.

* * * *

James, Yvonne, Big Ace and Sammy crept up to the ballroom door. James knew that it was risky, but it was now or never. He knew where all of the Terrorists were posted at, but wondered how he would get passed the door without getting everybody in the room killed. "We can't kick it in." Yvonne whispered.

"I know!" James said.

"Use your keys!" Sammy whispered.

"What?" James asked.

"You're the security, don't you got keys to all these doors?" Sammy reiterated.

James smiled and pulled out his keys quietly as he grabbed the master key, and slowly slid it into the lock.

Big Ace and Sammy moved to the side incase one of the Terrorist was standing by the door and started shooting. Yvonne was next to James listening thru the door, as James slowly turned the key to the lock, then grabbed his AR-15 rifle as he looked at Yvonne and smiled, then slowly twisted the door knob and pushed the door in real quick as he rolled into the room and shot the first Terrorist closes to the President. Yvonne was right behind him and shot the Terrorist that was on the stage, the other Terrorist let off a quick round of bullets at James catching him in the shoulder knocking him back as he fell back onto the carpet and Sammy and Big Ace both unloaded their clip into the Terrorist that shot James, watching his body dance against the back wall as the Tec-9 and AR-15 rifles ate thru his body.

When the smoke cleared, James was laying on his back holding his shoulder rolling in agony as the pain burned thru his shoulder. Yvonne jogged over to him and kneeled down on side of him feeling and looking for bullet wounds.

"Let me see?" Yvonne yelled as she looked at the wound. "Big Ace come and put pressure on his wound for me." Yvonne yelled. "Sammy get the security on the door." Sammy ran by the door and reloaded his Tec-9 then posted up. "Is everybody o'kay? Mr. President are you o'kay?" Yvonne asked as she ran over to the dead Terrorist and grabbed their guns from them.

"Yes I'm fine, but the Governor has been shot and lost a lot of blood." The President said.

Yvonne kneeled down and looked at the Governor and said. "I need you two to carry him." She pointed at two Leaders. "Mr. President here take this gun," and she handed him a Tec-9 rifle.

The India Prime Minister went to grab the other AR-15 rifle off the ground and Sammy said. "Wait muthafucka! What are you doing?"

"I'm going-tu help you guys!" The India Prime Minister said.

"Sammy what are you doing he's the India Prime Minister." Yvonne yelled.

"Move back let me get this! Fuck that shit Yvonne, this muthafucka ain't holding no guns around me. Not on my watch, I'll carry two guns....fuck that!" Sammy said firmly.

"He got a point!" Big Ace said as he helped James stand up.

"O'kay, James can you shoot?" Yvonne asked.

James pulled out his 45 automatic and said "I'm good."

"O'kay James you and Big Ace lead the way. I'll stay in the middle with the President and Sammy you take the back, and let's get the hell out of here."

"O'kay, ya'll follow us and keep your eyes open and heads low. Big Ace shoot to kill!" James said.

"Gotcha playa! We got ya'll. Let's roll out." Big Ace said as they started creeping down the hallway with their guns up.

Chapter 11

Abby Shakur look at his watch and said "It was a trick! They went after the President. Abuk, Akbar, Saul back to the ballroom quick." Abby said as they started running back toward the ballroom. Abby's comrades was spread out in a tactical format, and started running back from the lounge toward the elevator and stairwell, when one of the Terrorist got shot and flipped as he screamed and the other Terrorist stopped and turned, right when the SWAT Team member shot and hit the statute that was in front of him. He started shooting wildly as he screamed "police, police!" and Abby and Akbar looked as their comrade got ate up by a swarm of bullets dropping him dead.

"Come on let go!" Mr. Kerr hollered as Abby unloaded his 40 gloc at one of the SWAT Team Members, then him and Mr. Kerr ran inside the stairwell.

James and Big Ace was moving down the stairwell toward the second floor with the Leaders trailing close behind them, when a Terrorist turned the corner and as he was running, Big Ace lit him up with his AR-15 bullets that tore right thru him, killing him dead.

"They must know that we tricked them," James said as Big Ace shook his head.

The bottom door opened and a voice said "Not that way we got to get out of here. Come on this way!"

James and Big Ace ran down the stairwell to the lobby floor and heard footsteps running in the stairwell below them. "They went toward the basement," James said as he heard footsteps running toward the stairwell as the stairwell door swung open, James and Big Ace had their guns pointed at a SWAT Team member's head. James pushed Big Ace's AR-15 rifle right as Big Ace fired a spurt of bullets that hit the wall. The SWAT Team member's gun was trained on James head as James said, "We're on your side," and Yvonne peeped around the corner with her gun aimed at the SWAT Team member's head.

The SWAT member lowered his gun as two more SWAT Members appeared in the doorway. "We got the President of the United States here and the other Leaders. We need to get them up out of here now!" Yvonne said.

"Come on, follow us!" The SWAT Team Leader shouted.

James and Big Ace posted up as the President and the Leaders passed them by and they exited out of the stairwell. James looked at Yvonne, Big Ace and Sammy and said, "They ran into the basement and I'm going in after them!"

"You're in no condition to go after them." Yvonne argued.

"I'll be alright, get the President out of here, and I'll use the military radio to stay in touch." James said as he smiled at the President and saluted him, then ran down the stairwell.

Yvonne looked at Big Ace and Sammy and Big Ace said, "Alright, we'll go with him.

"Wait a minute, what do you mean we? I don't want to go down there. I'm trying to get out of here too!" Sammy replied.

"Come on man, quit acting like a bitch!" Big Ace said.

"Fuck you nigga, I ain't no bitch, if I die down here then I'mma hunt your ass for the rest of your life." Sammy said as they ran down the stairs.

Yvonne and the SWAT Team escorted the President and the other Leaders out of the Casino where the Secret Service, FBI and the Army were waiting.

"Ms. Bay, I'm glad to see that you've made it out. You did a splendid job." The Secret Service Captain said.

"Wait a minute, I got to go back! James, Big Ace and Sammy went after Abby Shakur and Mr. Kerr. They ran toward the basement and I got to go help them" Yvonne shouted.

"Wait a minute Yvonne, the SWAT Team can handle this now.

"No I have to go! That's my Team down there. I gotta go help them, that's my responsibility!" Yvonne said firmly.

"O'kay, you go with her!" The Secret Service Captain said as he pointed to three SWAT Members, and they shook their heads and ran alongside her.

* * * *

Big Ace and Sammy heard James 45 automatic shoot four times as they were creeping down the dark hallway in the lower basement. Big Ace looked at Sammy and said "Come on."

* * * *

James was creeping down the hallway as Abby Shakur jumped out at him, he was hiding behind some boxes. James was taken by surprise when Abby Shakur grabbed his gun arm and James let off four shots as they tussle for position. Abby hit James arm against the wall and the 45 automatic fell from his hand and dropped on the ground. Abby socked James in the face then kneed James in the stomach three times knocking the wind out of James as he fell to his knees. "Get the damn gun!" Abby hollered at Mr. Kerr as Mr. Kerr reached down and picked up the gun. "I told you that I would kill you if you tried to trick me." Abby said as he socked James in the face knocking him to the ground, then he kicked James in the face and James vision went blurry. "You will be remembered as the fool who died trying to play hero. Kerr, shoot this self-righteous bastard."

Mr. Kerr lifted the 45 automatic as James looked over at him and Mr. Kerr said, "sorry my friend."

Then James heard a loud gun shot as he closed his eyes and didn't feel no pain, he opened his eyes back up and saw Mr. Kerr on the ground, and his 45 automatic on the ground five feet away from him. Big Ace socked Abby in the face dropping him to the ground, while Sammy kicked Abby in the face knocking Abby on his back and Sammy started pistol whooping him with his big ass Desert Eagle that he just shot Mr. Kerr with. "You want to run around and kill innocent people and act crazy take this, and this is for little Scott bitch." Sammy said as he pistol whooped Abby Shakur.

"Sammy, Sammy, don't kill him" James shouted.

"Why not, he was gonna kill you?"

"Let the system deal with him!"

"I am the muthafucken system right now" Sammy yelled.

"There are families who want to see justice served." James said.

"You're lucky!" Sammy said as he searched Abby, then drugged him over by James.

Big Ace had Mr. Kerr in a choke hold as he lead him over to where James and Sammy was standing. "You should've known better," Sammy said as he socked Mr. Kerr in the eye.

Yvonne ran up with three SWAT Team Members and said, "Are you guys alright?"

James, Sammy and Big Ace faces were swollen from the ass whooping that they took and they looked at one another and started laughing. "We'll survive!" James said as they all started laughing.

The SWAT Team Members handcuffed Abby and Mr. Kerr and lead them out of the Casino as James and Yvonne followed and Sammy and Big Ace was close behind them.

"Damn it feels like I got to shit" Sammy whispered to Big Ace.

"Don't do it! Whatever you do, don't do it" Big Ace said as his eyes got big and he shook his head in a no manner.

As they entered the lobby police was everywhere. The General walked up to them and looked at Abby and Mr. Kerr and said, "I will make sure that you both get the electric chair for this. Lieutenant read them their rights."

"You have the right to remain silent. Anything you say can and will be used against you" The Lieutenant spoke as they escorted Abby Shakur and Mr. Kerr away.

"Your sacrifice and contribution to this country and the world abroad is immeasurable. You guys saved this country from a devastating ordeal, and we are deeply in debted to you!" The General stated as he stood and saluted James, Yvonne, Big Ace, and Sammy.

They looked around and all of the Law Officers was saluting them.

"I feel like Rambo right now" Sammy whispered as they all laughed.

"Thank you, it was an honor to serve our country." James boldly said.

"James, James how you doing young man?" The Captain of the police department asked as he walked up.

"I'm doing fine Sir, a little sore but I'll be alright." James responded as the paramedic's ran over and started catering to his bullet wound.

"I can imagine you look sore" The Captain said as they shook hands. You know, that Expedition truck that you called in during your Jade Abdul incident, got found! It was used to blow up the Police Station during this incident. Apparently, there was some type of connection between Abby Shakur and Mr. Jade Abdul. We got an APB out for Mr. Jade Abdul as we speak. You're an excellent Detective and we will be honored if you will come back to work for us and I personally will promote you to Lieutenant" The Captain said.

"Thank you, I have to think about it" James said as he cried out in pain "Ouch!" as the paramedic was cleaning his wound.

The FBI Agent walked up to James and said, "I would like to shake your hand Sir! That was the best police work that I have ever seen. We recovered the hundred and forty billion that was stolen from all of our banks. But it seem like we lost a few millions somewhere in limbo. Nevertheless, you stopped the biggest economical crash since 1929 Great Depression and save the President of the United States and a lot of other Leaders. You guys are American heroes." The FBI Agent excitedly said.

"Thank you Sir, do you know where they are keeping my sister and the other hostage that was rescued earlier?" James asked.

"Yes, they're in the big tent that we set up on the golf course, Michael can you take Mr. Pryor to the tent?"

"Yes Sir, Mr. Grand! This way Sir," the young FBI Agent said as he escorted James toward the entrance.

"James where are you going?" Big Ace asked as him and Sammy was surrounded by police agents as they joked about how they had to whoop ass to survive.

"I'm going out to the tent to meet up with my sister."

"Wait a minute we coming with you. Come on Sammy! We'll see ya'll later." Big Ace said as him and Sammy jogged over to James.

"What's wrong to many police around here?" James joked.

"I guess that you know me pretty well!" Big Ace smiled as Sammy gave him dap.

"James, James, tell them that I don't know nothing." Cin yelled as two police was escorting him out.

"Don't worry Cin, I got your back! They just got to interview you and do an investigation but I got you, don't worry."

"O'kay, James thank you!" Cin said as the police escorted him out.

Yvonne walked up to them and said, "I just wanted to thank you guys, you're the best Team that I ever had!"

"You're the baddest bitch I ever met too!" Sammy said.

"Well, I'll take that as a compliment!"

"Yvonne you know that Mr. Cin is innocent," said James.

"Yes I know, and I plan on putting that in my report. I guess that I'll see you guys later." Yvonne said.

"Hopefully!" James said as she hugged them all and smiled and walked away.

"I like her, she's hot!" Big Ace said as they walked out and got in the police car.

Two minutes later James, Big Ace and Sammy was walking into the tent as everybody turned and started applauding them. James, Big Ace and Sammy started smiling.

"I can get use to this!" Big Ace said as five beautiful Showgirls ran up to them hugging and thanking them.

Janet and Debbie ran into James arms, as he cried out in pain. They noticed his shoulder and started babying him.

"Are you o'kay baby?" Debbie asked.

"I am now!" James smiled as Debbie gave him a big wet kiss on the lips.

Janet said, "I like this one, she's a keeper," and they started giggling!

Eve ran up and James held out his good arm and gave her a big hug. "I knew that you'd make it out alright, thank you for saving my life."

"It was worth it," James said as she smiled back at him.

"You know that I can use a new body guard" Eve flirted.

"Well, I think I got my hands full right now." James said as he grabbed hold of Debbie's hand.

"O'kay, but if you're ever in Canada, then call me! I'll take you both out for a good time." Eve said as she gave James a piece of paper with her phone number on it.

"Will do, and you take care of yourself o'kay"

"O'kay," she said as she kissed James on the cheek and walked away.

"James what's up buddy!" Bill said as he walked up and shook James hand.

"Bill, what's good man! Let me talk to you for a minute. Excuse us ladies," James said as he pulled Bill to the side.

"What's up buddy?" Bill asked.

"Listen Bill, I know that some of the money that was stolen from those banks accounts came up missing, and only one person alive had access to those electronic accounts. So I know that you took it, because you're the expertise! Now I'm gonna ask you one question? Is there any way that they would be able to find out that you have it?"

"Have what James, I didn't...?"

"Don't lie to me Bill, I'll turn your ass in right now!" James threatened.

"O'kay, o'kay.... No it can't come back on me. I put the money in an overseas bank account that I set-up awhile back, when I transfer any money into that account it's transferred automatically into another bank's account at a different location within an hour. So they will never find it. Believe me, I know my stuff…I'm a professional hacker!" Bill proudly confused!

"How much did you take?"

"Something little!"

"How little?" James said.

"About Six hundred and Seventeen million," Bill said.

"Damn, what's my cut?" James asked.

"Serious?"

"Hell yeah!"

"O'kay, I'll give you three hundred million but no one can know"

"Scout's honor!" James said as he gave a sinister laugh.

"James how long before we can get out of here? We got plans!" Big Ace said as him and Sammy was standing next to five gorgeous Showgirls.

"I'm sure that they want to interview us, so let me go and see. Cause I got to go to the hospital and get this big ass hole in my shoulder sowed up and I got plans too."

James said as he smiled at Debbie, then walked over to the Lieutenant who was standing at the entrance of the tent.

"It feels good to be a hero" Sammy said.

"It's gonna be even better being a baller!" Big Ace said as they gave each other daps.

Epilogue

Three months after the Terrorist's incident James, Janet and James fiancée Debbie all started a non-profit organization for the victim family members of the Gold Stallion Terrorist attack. The non-profit organization received over twelve million dollars in donations from people from all over the world, not including a two hundred million dollars donation that they received anonymously, from a unknown overseas account. James, Janet and Debbie made sure that all of the children of the people who died in the tragic Terrorist attack, received a two hundred thousand dollar college fund, and a fifty thousand dollar trust account for when they turned twenty-one. Then they donated twenty million dollars to the Arizona Police Department for a new state of the art precinct.

Life couldn't be better as James took Debbie and Janet on a trip to the Bahamas, to enjoy some peace and tranquility with the two beautiful ladies in his life. James was laying next to Debbie and Janet on the twenty foot yacht that he rented when his cell phone rang.

"James speaking" James said as he answered his phone.

"James what's up buddy, how are you enjoying the Bahamas my man?" Bill who was on the other end of the phone said.

"How did you know that I was in the Bahamas?"

"James you know my craft! It's my job to stay informed, as long as they got computers and computerized I-phones, then I'm gonna always be ahead of the game." Bill laughed.

"I feel you bro! And I'm having the time of my life. How about you?"

"I'm out here in Germany enjoying the other side of the world. I just brought a new Bugatti and hit 170 mph on the Autobahn, pure sex!"

"I bet it is, but doesn't that car go something like 220 mph?"

"Yeah, but I punked out! A little old lady flew by me in a Ferrari Spider doing around 200 mph, and it really made me feel like a punk." They both laughed. "Anyway, I seen what you did with the non-profit thang and that was real big of you!"

"Well life has a way of touching us all in mysterious ways!"

"I feel you on that! And by the way thank you for the invitation to the wedding, I wouldn't miss it for the world."

"It would be a pleasure to see you there." James said.

"You and the wify have to come out to my mansion in Paris and let me take you both shopping as a wedding present."

"Sounds good!"

"And bring that fine sister of yours too, so I can show her how a real Baller plays." They both laughed.

"Let me find out that you're trickin' now! James joked.

"Oh, it's not considered trickin' when you got money....it's called ballin! And I'm a franchise playa'!"

"You're crazy" James laughed and looked over at Janet and Debbie and said, "Bill is inviting all of us to spend the weekend in Paris with him and he said he wants to take us on a shopping spree.

"Let's go!" They shouted.

"I guess it's a date then, tell me when it's convenient for you and I'll send my new Lear Jet to come and pick you up!"

"Will do Baller!" They laughed.

"O'kay, have a nice trip and holler back soon, O'kay!"

"Later! (Click)

"Look James Dolphins!" Debbie said as they watched the Dolphins play in the sunset.

* * * *

"O'kay Roger, thank you for letting me put them flowers in the lounge where my friend got killed at!"

"No problem Mr. Sammy, I understand and you have my condolences" The night guard to the empty Casino said.

Big Ace came out of the restroom and said, "that chili that I ate didn't agree with my stomach. I advise you not to go in the restroom for about ten minutes." Big Ace joked.

"You don't have to worry about that Mr. Ace, I can imagine. You guys have a nice day." The old white guard said as he escorted them to the front entrance and let them out.

They walked to Sammy new customized Range Rover truck and jumped in. "Did you get it? Was it still there?" Sammy asked as Big Ace pulled out the leather black bag from up underneath his arm pit, as he open up his black leather jacket.

"Of course I got it playa!"

"We're ballin!!" They said in unison. As Sammy started up the truck and cut up his music as Rick Ross the Boss echoed thru the speakers, and they drove away with a big smile on their faces.

The End

Ghetto Games 1 & 2,
they are the hottest urban faction tales written and a
must read for anyone who enjoys the mind twisting
drama of the ghetto street life and passion that feed our
ambitions to struggle against all odds.

Ghetto Games II *"The Ghetto Saga Continues"*

This is the coldest and realest west coast gangster street classic that has ever been written. "If you like that west coast gangsta street shit… then you will love this!
Now available in paperback on Amazon.com & Ghetto Theory.com

GHETTO GAMES III

GHETTO THEORY
PUBLISHING PRESENT'S

G. PRINCE

The ghetto games continue in the
deadliest games ever played; a bloody game of revenge!

Revenge is the definition of Ghetto Games, as the three young rawest West Coast Kingpins, find themselves fighting a deadly battle against the worse enemies that they could ever want to face... Some scandalous, crooked ass cops from the L.A.P.D.

This is part three from the coldest West Coast gangsta tale ever told; Ghetto Games." A guaranteed page turner that is street certified and gangsta approved. The sequel continues!

DOUBLE
TROUBLE

SMILE NOW.... DIE LATER

G. PRINCE
GHETTO THEORY PUBLISHING

This book is rated triple X for the extreme violent contents that has been realistically conveyed through the un-censorships that reflect the true urban struggles, and realities of the ghetto games.

Money, sex, murder, betrayal, drugs, and revenge only spells one thing, "Natural Born Gangster"

**LOOK FOR *GHETTO THEORY PUBLISHING*
LATEST NEW RELEASES IN BOOK STORES AND
FOR PURCHASE ON**

www.ghettotheory.com

www.Amazon.com
www.Smashword.com
www.Book Daily.com

*Now available in paperback on Amazon.com &
Ghetto Theory.com*

GHETTO THEORY PUBLISHING
Presents

Ghetto Games

Ghetto Games II, "the saga continues."

Am I My Sister's Keeper?

Natural Born gangster

Rules of the Street Game that Every Hustler Should Know...!

Look for *"Menage A' Trois"*

Featuring a new Author :
Madam Princess

Welcome to the underworld, where fantasies
become reality for one night, and desires and fetishes
are fed with greed and lust!
Welcome to "Menage A' Trois"

www.ingramcontent.com/pod-product-compliance
Lightning Source LLC
Chambersburg PA
CBHW071238130626
46556CB00003B/1059